Ezzedine C. Fishere is an acclaimed Egyptian writer, academic, and diplomat. He has written numerous successful and best-selling novels and he also writes political articles for Arabic, English, and French news outlets. He currently teaches at Dartmouth College in the US.

John Peate has studied Arabic in Algeria, Morocco, Egypt, Syria, and Oman, as well in the UK, and has a PhD in Arabic linguistics. He has translated the works of numerous Arab authors, has been a university teacher and a BBC journalist, and now works for the US Embassy in London as a media analyst.

D1407701

Embrace on Brooklyn Bridge

Ezzedine C. Fishere

Translated by
John Peate

hoopoe
AN IMPRINT OF AUC PRESS

SPOTLIGHT
ON RIGHTS

This book has been published under the Spotlight on Rights initiative of the Abu Dhabi International Book Fair

First published in 2017 by
Hoopoe
113 Sharia Kasr el Aini, Cairo, Egypt
420 Fifth Avenue, New York, 10018
www.hoopoefiction.com

Hoopoe is an imprint of the American University in Cairo Press
www.aucpress.com

Exclusive distribution outside Egypt and North America by I.B.Tauris & Co Ltd., 6 Salem Road, London, W4 2BU

Dar el Kutub No. 14201/16
ISBN 978 977 416 819 2

Dar el Kutub Cataloging-in-Publication Data

Fishere, Ezzedine C.
　　　Embrace on Brooklyn Bridge / Ezzedine C. Fishere.—Cairo: The American University in Cairo Press, 2017.
　　　　　p.　　　cm.
　　　　　ISBN 978 977 416 819 2
　　　　　1. Arabic Fiction — Translation into English
　　　　　892.73

1　2　3　4　5　　21　20　19　18　17

Designed by Adam el-Sehemy
Printed in the United States of America

1

The Book of Darwish

It had been his favorite chair for years, and yet he couldn't sit comfortably in it. His eyes hurt. Words were jumbled and pages merged into one another. Darwish lifted his watch to his squinting eyes. Five. Three hours until the guests arrived. Youssef was due at seven. Darwish had told him to take the subway, because the streets would be jammed. He'd be late if he got a taxi like he usually did. The remark seemed to irritate Youssef, but Darwish couldn't see why his son had gotten annoyed. He needed him there at least an hour before the guests. He was supposed to have come in the morning to oversee Kitty getting the birthday party ready. But he'd called the day before, saying he wanted to catch up with some old New York colleagues, so he'd check in with Kitty by phone and come at seven. Check in by phone! Well, that's if he even remembered to charge the damn thing. He really needed to speak to him before the guests arrived.

It looked like Kitty had done a good job. He'd passed by her downstairs an hour ago to check she was on top of everything. She'd gone out afterward to buy a few things. Three hours to go. No time for work of any real value, like writing. He had tried to use the time for reading, but his eyes were really hurting. He was dismayed he was wasting time now while he'd be pressed for time later, after the party. Why had no one invented a device to which you could upload spare time and download it later? These three hours, for example.

The guests would get there at eight, and wouldn't leave until eleven thirty. The joke was that Salma, the guest of honor, the birthday girl, wasn't coming. She had been running late, gotten the wrong train, and was going to turn up at midnight, after everyone else had gone. He asked himself for the thousandth time: what was it with these kids? Where had he gone wrong with them? Maybe it was genetic. He knew he shouldn't worry about it so much. If that's how they were, why not leave them to it? Let them become the kind of people they wanted to be: people who missed their appointments, missed trains, and lived in chaos. Leave them to enjoy blissful ignorance and the comfort of failure.

Youssef wasn't going to stick around for long. He was leaving in the morning, so there was no point making life difficult over him being late. Better to let things go peacefully for once, he thought to himself. Same with Salma. She would only be in New York a few more days, and he wouldn't see her again after that. Leave her with some good memories. He swore to himself he'd make it happen. So what would he do with these three hours, then? He had to finish the book proposal and submit it by the end of the week. He still had some thinking to do about that, and a whole heap of writing. But he had to sort out all of his books too, before the movers came. The house had to be cleared by the end of the month; in less than two weeks, in other words.

He gave up on the idea of reading, put the book aside, and laid his glasses on the table. The doctor had told him not to strain his eyes. If they started hurting, that was his cue to stop. He began brooding again. Why hadn't Salma caught the morning train? What a silly girl she was. She knew damn well this whole party was for her. The guests would be there at eight. Hellos, how-are-yous, that kind of thing, would take half an hour, then Kitty would bring the food in at eight thirty. Eating that late was hard on his poor digestive system. His insides were as tough as old leather these days. He'd normally make

2

do with a little yogurt, but it'd be a bit strange not to dine with his guests. Of course he'd eat with them. And, yes, of course he'd be awake until one in the morning trying to digest it. That would mean not enough sleep, unless he slept in until nine. Which was impossible; he had an appointment with his lawyer at eight thirty.

He was mad at himself. Why had he gotten himself into hosting this party anyway? If only he had invited them for lunch on the weekend instead. But Kitty wasn't free on weekends, and his idiotic little granddaughter wanted to visit DC before she went back to Egypt. Ah, what the hell, he thought. We are where we are. He'd just have to get up at seven and spend the rest of the day tired and grouchy. What else could he do?

He couldn't read, write, or do anything meaningful in those three hours. It occurred to him to sort through the old bookcases. Maybe he could use the time till Youssef showed up sorting through them. Then he could sit down with Youssef for a little while, hear what was happening with him until the guests arrived. Yes, that was it. He'd sort through his old books. If it had been left to him, he'd have taken all of them with him to the new place, but the cabin was too small. He knew, of course, that he wouldn't actually need any of them, but they had a special place in his heart.

He had arranged with the realtor's office for someone to fix some more bookshelves to the cabin walls, but there was still not enough room. They had worked out the exact amount of space, as well as the number of books he could take; he'd have to get rid of three thousand before he moved in. He had sifted through his old university books the week before, and donated a thousand to the postgraduates' study room. They wouldn't read a single one of them, of course, but it was better than shelves lying empty, or plastered with student posters. So he had two thousand books to get rid of in a week. He couldn't donate any more to the university, the student union, or any other organization in the whole of the United States for that matter. Most of them were in Arabic, and their educational worth was limited. That was why he kept them in the most private section of his library.

These were the books he had bought in his youth. Some were naïve introductions to theater, painting, sculpture, written by unknown authors who had plagiarized foreign books, and printed by government-owned publishing houses in the Sixties. Some were generalist social critiques written by journalists who understood neither criticism nor society. Some were anthologies by long-dead poets who probably hadn't ever had an audience. He had bought most of these books when he was in high school, or in his early university years. There were others he'd bought while he was working on his doctoral thesis and first started teaching: his Cairo University days. The only value in these books was the part they had played in his life. They were worthless to anyone else.

Youssef and Leila were shocked that he was selling the house. Youssef had asked him what was behind the sudden decision. And he had tried to dodge the question, calling it a seventieth birthday present to himself. Darwish's non-answer was not enough for Youssef, who pursued the point, asking if he was moving into a retirement home. Darwish laughed, sort of. "Over my dead body," he said, before changing the subject. When Darwish called Leila in Egypt, she asked him flat out if he needed money. He had dodged that one too. He didn't want an argument. He said he was bored with the house, but she snapped back that it was the one place they all had shared memories of. He said again that he was bored of the place, then realized he had repeated himself, and quickly added that their shared memories would follow them wherever they were. Leila didn't even pretend to understand. She was brutally honest about how unhappy she was about it, and said she'd rather he left things as they were. He archly asked what she planned to do with her house of memories, since she wasn't likely to

4

spend any time in it. She hadn't visited for two years. Then Leila again, then him again, and then the conversation wound inevitably down the same old path of incomprehension and suppressed anger on both sides. He changed the subject, then she changed the subject, and it ended up with both promising to meet soon, with neither of them really knowing where or when that would happen.

Youssef, after getting no straight answer from his father to his questions, decided to come home one last time, also to see his niece Salma. "Oh, now he remembers she's in New York! She's been here three weeks!" Darwish welcomed the visit, but without enthusiasm. He never knew what to do with him when he came. Youssef would disappear into silence most of the time. He'd grant his father's stream of questions the odd curt answer. In the end, Darwish would give up asking. Then there'd be silence on both sides. Youssef would spend the rest of his time there wandering around the big old house. He might watch a little TV or work on his computer till it was time to leave. That was how he'd been since he was three, when Darwish had split up with his mother; he was the same forty years later. Youssef asked Darwish if he needed anything from Montreal, and Darwish asked for bagels. He couldn't think of anything else. Darwish had tried to give Youssef his old books, saying on the phone that he had two thousand he needed to part with, and casually asking if he wanted any of them. Youssef laughed, then thanked him and offered to store them in his basement.

Darwish stood contemplating his old bookcase, looking at books he hadn't laid eyes on for years. He had walked past them hundreds of times without paying them any attention. It was hard to look at them now he'd decided to get rid of them. It was like he was tossing away parts of himself. These books had helped shape him, make him the man he was—or, more precisely, the man he had been in his thirties before he had come to the States. He suddenly wondered if he had actually changed at all since then. He knew he had, but wondered whether he had taken a good look at himself since that time, or whether he had simply flipped the pages without noticing the changes. He wondered whether he'd just shelved everything like the works on that old bookcase.

He continued to sort through them, wondering why he hadn't told his children the real reason he was selling. Why not tell them he was putting his affairs in order before the final departure? "Advanced pulmonary cancer." That's what the medics had called it. When he refused chemotherapy, the doctor had told him bluntly that he wouldn't live long. A year, maybe two. Darwish replied that two years without chemo was better than five years with it. The doctor could tell his mind was made up, and told him his current lifestyle wouldn't give him much time without the therapy. Darwish said he was ready to change his lifestyle. The doctor said it meant he'd have to stop teaching, stop reading newspapers, stop following the news—stop anything that could cause stress. He should move upstate where the air, food, and water were better, healthier. The cancer would keep spreading, but the metastasis in his lungs would slow down a little. Darwish didn't need to think about it for long. He'd dreamed all his life of living in a remote little cabin in the woods. Pure air, clean water, greenery. Best of all, he would be able to get away from other human beings. He accepted the doctor's advice right away, and his realtor contacted him a week later to say they had the very thing he was looking for. A cabin overlooking a medium-sized lake in New York State's northeastern mountains bordering Vermont. It wasn't far from Syracuse, which had a state-of-the-art hospital where he could have his checkups. Darwish made a quick visit, and found that the cabin was right on the lakeside, surrounded by towering trees and thick vegetation. There was no other building as far as the eye could see. He made up his mind then and there, standing in front of the cabin, gazing out at the lake's surface.

The timing was bad. The semester was about to begin and abandoning his teaching duties so suddenly would not go down well, but he went ahead with it anyway. The faculty head, whom Darwish had taught twenty-five years ago, was shocked. His old teacher had given no sign of intent to retire. Quite the opposite, in fact: Darwish was immersed in departmental development plans, and still led his research team with the same rigor he had applied for years. Darwish gave no explanation, confirming only his intention to go. He did not elaborate. The faculty head tried to talk him out of it, but Darwish left no scope for negotiation. In the space of a few days, and after three or four talks with the senior administration of the university, Professor Darwish Bashir put an end to his distinguished, half-century-long academic career. In the weeks that followed, he wound up the rest of his commitments in New York, sold the house, and began planning the simpler, more modest life his doctor had prescribed.

Why couldn't he tell Youssef and Leila any of this? Or his old colleague and former student? Why couldn't he tell anyone he knew, in fact? Because he didn't want anyone making a fuss. He hated drama. He hated having to play the victim, be the object of people's sympathy. What good was having someone profess their pity for you? What good was that to you? And then he would have to take on the role of the brave and tragic figure, to make their sorrow easier for them. No, thanks. No, he didn't want any part in that. He didn't want acquaintances showering him with their sympathy, genuine or fake. He didn't want to waste his final days. His doctors had advised him to avoid whatever made him irritable, and that kind of sympathy was sure to irritate him. The truth was he didn't see any of this, or what lay ahead, as a tragedy. On the contrary, he felt relieved when the doctors told him. He even had to suppress a smile until he was safely alone. He felt fate had handed him a final victory: allowing him to go while he was at the top of his game. Death was supposed to come suddenly, but he'd been given advance notice. He put on a tragic face, because that's what you were supposed to do, but really he felt relieved, like a heavy load had been lifted.

He realized he wouldn't leave much behind. He would die like everyone else did. Those who really loved him would remember him fondly; the rest would remember him the way they wanted. This didn't matter to him. Darwish was seventy years old, and it actually felt like a blessing to know how much time he had left. It was a chance to put his affairs in order, with his own two hands, and to do what he had forgotten or been too lazy to do. From that time onward, he wouldn't do anything he didn't want to. He would flatter no one. He would spend no time on people he didn't like. He wouldn't make compromises or long-term plans. There was no long term anymore. He would do all the things he'd put off. He'd live in his remote log cabin on a lake in the woods or the mountains. He'd read books he'd never had time to pick up before. He'd write the book he'd always wanted to write: on the future of the Arabs. He'd spent his whole life studying Arab history. He had always dreamed of writing about their future, but his natural cautiousness prevented him. Now there was no point in being cautious. He would draft the book proposal and meet with the publisher early next week. Once he was in the cabin, he would begin writing.

He called Leila in Cairo and cajoled her into sending Salma to stay with him for a month. He tried to persuade Leila herself to visit, but she flatly refused, like she had done for years. He wanted Salma to come so that he could see her for the last time, but he also wanted to drag her out of that shell her demented mother kept her in. He wanted to rid her of the shackles she wore in Egypt. She might even be tempted to finish her studies in the States, and maybe settle down here afterward. You never know, he might succeed in rescuing her from the miserable future her mother had in mind for her.

When Youssef announced he was coming too, Darwish organized this birthday party, inviting a few friends and relatives. He decided to invite everyone he was close to in the US so that they could see Salma, and so that he could see them for the last time and sort out a few practical matters before he died. He wanted to give a few of them money, to help some of them out with their jobs, and to bid all of them farewell. Then he'd see his lawyer at eight thirty in the morning, get it all down on paper, in a will, and arrange the funeral. After that, he'd move to the cabin and devote himself to writing his last book. He would have liked to have kept Kitty on but couldn't, so he had arranged for a maid to look after him at the cabin. She'd fix his meals, go shopping, drive him to Syracuse when it got too much for him, that kind of thing. He bought a little boat and looked forward to sitting and gazing out over the silence of the lake, soundless and motionless but for the lapping of little waves on the prow. He might learn to fish. He bought a big TV screen and huge speakers, the kind he'd refused to buy for years because they were too pricey. He bought a pickup truck too— just right for the terrain around the cabin. Everything was ready for the move. All he had to do now was to sort out those books.

He didn't recognize it at first: Albert Hourani's *A History of the Arab Peoples*. His eyes lingered on it for a few moments, unable to recall where it had come from or what it was about. Then, in a single instant, the past forty years hit him. There were Jane and Zeinab, standing in front of him in two different houses, in two different eras. He was overwhelmed, and things began to spin around him. Dropping the book on the floor, he grabbed hold of the bookcase, but his unsteadiness didn't ease. He knew that dizziness well, and that it wouldn't pass quickly. He tried to gingerly lower himself to the floor, but the dizziness was too strong. He lost his balance and, though he tried to clutch the shelving, slipped and fell onto the wool rug. He waited for moment, prone there on the floor, then tried moving his arms and legs. Everything seemed to be where it should be. Nothing broken. Not yet. He crawled slowly to the bookcase, slumped against it, and sat catching his breath. He thought to himself that he had been smart to insist on wooden floors after all. Had he followed Zeinab's plan and installed tiles he would have definitely broken a bone. He often had these dizzy spells. None of the doctors could treat them. They told him it was because his blood pressure would suddenly drop, but they didn't know why. What was the use of these goddamn doctors who told you what was wrong with you without being able to fix it?

He sat slumped on the rug, contemplating his study with its elegant, neatly made, brown wooden shelves. Thin white drapes hung over the wide window, the tree in the street visible beyond them. Not a sound got into the room through that double-glazed window. The wood of the window frame matched that of the shelves. There was not a speck of dust on the books. Good job, Kitty, he thought. He looked at the book that had fallen onto the floor beside him. Where had it been all those years? How could it have been there all that time without catching his eye? His faintness subsided little by little. He inched toward the book on all fours, grabbed it, and maneuvered himself back to the bookcase. He smiled as he flicked through Hourani's pages.

He had bought it in London, but not because he had hoped to learn about the history of the Arabs. He was already an expert on that. He had bought it for Jane, his British girlfriend. It was an easy read and a good introduction for those who didn't know any Arab history and wanted to get a lot out of one book. Hourani started with the emergence of Islam and its teachings, then its spread beyond the Arabian Peninsula, through the various eras, the different dynasties, the ebbs and flows of Arab politics, until he reached the modern age. All this in a few hundred pages. He gave it to her as a gift, jokingly suggesting it would cure her of her ignorance.

Though he had spent five years in London writing up his doctoral thesis, he hadn't met Jane there, but in Cairo, which surprised their small circle of friends. Jane was tall, slim, shapely, and beautiful, with long chestnut-brown hair, which she would either let hang around her shoulders or pin up with whatever was to hand, normally a pencil. She had come to Cairo for a year to learn Arabic, on some scholarship or another. She grew to love the city in all its chaos and ended up settling there. They gradually got to know each other, and grew closer until they ended up more or less living together in an apartment in Giza, behind the zoo.

The thought of marrying Jane had occurred to him early on: she had many of the qualities he sought in a partner. But something about her unnerved him, so he didn't tell Leila or Youssef about her until he was sure of their relationship.

He traveled with her to Britain to visit her parents, who lived on the outskirts of Glasgow. They walked to the riverbank where she had played as a girl, gazing across the endless pastures. She took him to the local pub, where throngs of young men had pestered her as a teenager. And they met all the neighbors who wanted to see "this Egyptian Jane has fetched back."

Jane was a good-hearted, decent sort of person, but her relationship with Egypt was confused. She told Darwish when they first met how much she loved the Egyptian people's good-naturedness, and their warmth and humanity. She found something in them that she had felt lacking from her life in Britain. He laughed to himself, being someone who actually loved the cool standoffishness of the British, finding in their respect for privacy something he lamented as sorely missing from Egyptian life. They found themselves in reversed positions, as he criticized she defended Egyptian life and people: "Yes, she is lying. From a legal point of view, she's lying. But it's not a real lie"; "This is not a weakness, it's caution"; "No that's not nepotism, it's really just an expression of gratitude";

"It's absolutely not a class thing; it's a different view of roles and responsibilities."

He never accepted any of her excuses, never accepted that different rules applied to Arabs. Arabs were not a corrupt offshoot of the rest of humanity. The same rules and moral standards applied to them as to anyone else in the world. Saying anything else was patronizing trash masquerading as sympathy. To accept a lie from an Arab but no one else meant you saw a fundamental weakness in them that the rest of humankind didn't suffer from. It was treating them as if they were granted permission to be irrational. He told her this, time and time again. Her indulgence of Egyptians and their shortcomings began to aggravate him. He asked her to read their history to understand why they were just like any other people, and how they had ended up the way they had. She would then see that indulging their faults was not the solution. Treating them like responsible grown-ups was. She tolerated, even reveled in their backwardness. Jane said she didn't have the time to immerse herself in Arab history like that. Enter Albert Hourani. When he gave her the book, she seemed pleased. She did start reading it, but soon gave up, saying it was boring and that she preferred to learn through mixing with people.

But she didn't learn through mixing with people. In fact, she slid deeper into "idiotic tourist syndrome," as Darwish diagnosed it. This was an ongoing argument between them, as she believed the real problem was that his way of thinking barred him from recognizing any of the complications unique to Egypt. He would protest that he was born of Egypt's soil, but he could tell the difference between complications and plain old bad behavior. In his view, Egyptians needed re-education. Whether it was because of their poverty or ignorance or poor education made no difference to him; the upshot was a deterioration in their moral codes. She would counter that he was the victim of his Western education, which had planted in him this naïve idea that people could be reformed through argument or appeals to conscience. That's why he fought with everyone all the time: because he preached at them instead of trying to understand them. He would laugh and ask sarcastically whether that was an insult or a compliment, and her face would redden.

On one occasion, she gave the example of the passport official who had been dragging his feet over her visa papers until she had quietly slipped him fifty Egyptian pounds. Darwish had protested at the time: "That's exactly the kind of petty bribery that has built the grand edifice of corruption in this country."

She tried to remind him that there was more to it than that, adding, "The state pays its employees a nominal salary, knowing it's not enough to get by on and that they will top it up from those who need services and favors."

"That's just an excuse."

"But that's how things really are. You can't claim right or wrong when that's how life is here."

He gave her a condescending smile, patted her shoulder, and said, "That is a perfect example of your confused logic. Right is right and wrong is wrong. The only people who confuse the two are the morally bankrupt."

"What you call immorality is actually just a different type of morality, with its own beauty."

That really irked him. He felt he was involved with an imbecile; all she needed was to wear rags and run after a Sufi nutcase. He accused her of compensating for her failure to integrate into British life by taking a stance that allowed her to feel superior. She was a victim of her own mythmaking about the mysterious Orient. She countered that he was, in fact, infatuated with the myth of Western order. He looked at her with almost complete despair. Then he said there was a seminar he wanted to catch, and left.

After this familiar argument, their life would return to its calm normality.

He was teaching at Cairo University, a short walk from their house. She was working all the time with various projects for an assortment of civil society groups, from helping garbage collectors to looking after street kids. But the differences between them put an end to their shared social life. He saw no point in involving her in his problems, whether those related to his work or to his fraught relationship with his children and their mother, which had begun to take up a greater part of his life. Everything seemed to require explanations and discussions, and produced unbridgeable disagreements. Darwish confessed to Jane one day that he found it hard to deal with his children. Youssef was stubborn and would take no direction from him, either ignoring what he said or pretending not to understand. Leila was defensive all the time, of herself and her mother, whenever he made even the mildest remark. She was forever edgy, even hostile at times. Jane asked him why he insisted on commenting on everything his kids did. He responded that he expected better from them. He couldn't change their mother, who was the cause of all this bad behavior, so he had to use whatever time he had with them to set them right. Jane suggested he should learn to accept them as they were, rather than trying to reform them. He tried to explain his objections, but she didn't understand. She just kept repeating herself until he gave up on the conversation. From then on, Darwish avoided the subject, and started avoiding other subjects. In the end, the things they couldn't talk to each other about dwarfed everything else. Silence became the norm. Their life together didn't last long after that.

He smiled while recalling it all. He wiped the grime off the book's white jacket and wondered if he could really throw it out, into the abyss. He had used this book to measure the women in his life. Would it really end up in the recycling or, worse, in the garbage? He pictured the words gradually paling as the pages of the book were pulped, till there was nothing left but plain white.

*

His back hurt. Was it possible that such a little fall could have hurt him this much? Sitting on the floor was painful. Coping with wooden flooring was not as easy as he had thought. It was the first time he'd sat on it, of course. And putting it in had caused a lot of heartache between him and Zeinab. Why had installing wooden floors mattered so much?

It was close to six o'clock, and he hadn't sorted through anything like enough of the books. Failing to make the most of his time like this irked him, but he comforted himself with the thought that he would have all the time he needed once he was in his cabin. He had to put all these memories, as well as that damned book, to one side. He could sort through a few hundred before Youssef arrived. He wondered about giving the book to Youssef. He didn't like reading, though—never had. Darwish thought he had deliberately chosen a career in international relief organizations so as not to have to do much reading. After all, handing out sacks of flour to the needy didn't require much background research. If Darwish asked him to take the book, he would, but what would he do with it? Perhaps he'd give it one of his girlfriends, maybe even his wife-to-be, to read. Not that Darwish had ever met a girlfriend, or heard anything about one. Had Darwish destroyed his son's faith in women, or was it unfair to blame himself? It could be Youssef's silent moping that drove women away. Or maybe his hatred of reading. Or maybe he fell in love with women who gave him Hourani to read, and then dumped him.

Darwish turned the book over in his hands. He didn't think he could bear to part with it.

Zeinab had read it, or had started it, at least. She spent long years poring over it but read incredibly slowly. She died before she finished it. Darwish had known from the first year that she never would get to the end of it and began to lose hope in her altogether. The poor woman died before she'd got past the

Mamluks. Why did remembering that make him smile now? He didn't know. The truth was he hadn't understood much about his impulses regarding Zeinab, and that included what made him marry her. She had been so far removed from his idea of the sort of woman he wanted to be with. No one, including himself, could work out why he and Zeinab had gotten married. Leila couldn't, Youssef couldn't. His friends and colleagues couldn't work it out. Even Zeinab herself couldn't.

He met her in the hospital where she worked, when his mother was being treated there. Zeinab was nice, slim, attractive, clever. She would apologize for herself all the time, and was shy, clamming up if anyone talked to her. He had tried a few times, but she was very much the quiet type. The more he tried to draw her into conversation, the quieter she became. She told him later that she cursed her silence every time he left her office and thought over all the many things she should have said to him. She always swore to herself not to do it the next time, but she always did. That's the way things continued until Darwish's mother was discharged from the hospital. After a few months, however, his mother became housebound, so he contacted the hospital manager and asked him to send a junior doctor to examine her at home, and suggested Zeinab. They saw each other once a week at his home when she came to see to his mother. Things developed pretty quickly between them after that.

He felt very attracted to her, but was also well aware that there were twenty years between them, and twenty other things. As their relationship grew, he would harp on about the age gap, but she would laugh it off, saying it was him who would end up going to her funeral. Age wasn't the only gap between them, however. He was quick-witted; she was ponderous. He was focused and organized; she was airy and capricious. He was thick-skinned; she was sensitive. He was ambitious and determined; she was easily sidetracked and generally quite negative. He was focused on the world of ideas;

16

she was not. He was proud to the point of arrogance; she was humble to the point of impassivity. He was image-conscious; she was resigned to other people trampling all over her. He loathed people, but forced himself to engage with them. She loved people, but was distant. He was a manipulator; she had no agenda. He was fiery; she was gentle. He was life's expert, she its novice. Darwish wasn't sure they would last, or what, if anything, would hold them together, but he found himself compellingly drawn to her.

One day he decided to follow his heart. He had been ill and was feverish. He woke up to find her dabbing his forehead with a damp towel. In his drowsiness, he grabbed her hand and kissed it. She stroked his hair and kissed his hand tenderly. She asked him directly if he loved her, and he smiled and said, "Seems that way." She smiled too, and told him she had loved him from the very first. She didn't know how she'd cope when he left her. He asked why she assumed he would. She said she knew she wasn't good enough for him, and that he would surely leave her one day. He smiled and told her that she should truly hope so, because he was hard work to live with, a little tiresome, and a little obsessive. She was quiet for a time, then said slowly and purposefully that she knew that, but it didn't scare her. He leaned over to her and asked if she'd marry him. She kissed him and said simply, "Yes."

What had made him marry her? Leila asked the question angrily, Youssef skeptically. Incredulous friends asked too. His way with words helped him craft an answer for each one. He used the answers with Zeinab too, when she asked. And she asked him often, as though testing how sincere he was. He never found an answer to convince himself, though. But they had gotten married nonetheless.

It wasn't long before he got the call from a university in New York. His standing as a serious historian had grown substantially and he'd published in various prestigious journals. New York called, and it didn't take him long to answer.

He had left London after his doctorate, and had been back in Egypt for seven years. That was long enough to convince him there was no point staying in his country of birth. He'd gone home because he'd felt a sense of responsibility to his family and to his country. But seven years of teaching feeble-minded students who understood nothing and had no desire to learn changed his mind. Seven years of failure in reforming the department, despite all the promises made, all the money spent, and all the grandiose statements issued, convinced him trying was pointless. Seven years of sterile debates with fellow academics and writers who couldn't link their premises to their conclusions convinced him to leave. Seven years of dealing with a society hooked on its own hang-ups, a prisoner of its victim mentality, and hostile to anyone who suggested it needed to get out of the mess it was in convinced him that this was a doomed nation. Nothing and no one could rescue it. So he decided to save himself instead. Zeinab was more than happy to leave an Egypt she felt suffocated by. Leila, however, wouldn't leave her friends, and decided to stay with her mother. And, of course, she railroaded Youssef into doing the same. Darwish left with Zeinab, leaving his children behind, but determined to lure them to the States later.

Life in New York suited him perfectly. The academic atmosphere at the university was all that he had hoped it would be. He settled down, and his academic work flourished, even shone.

Zeinab found it tough. For a start, she had to take all kinds of exams to get her medical qualifications recognized in the States, even though she had practiced in one of Cairo's major hospitals. This siphoned much of her time and energy and took her away from everything else she needed to do to acclimatize. It affected her psychologically, and also had an impact on their home life and marriage. He didn't like this, not one bit, and was quite open about his displeasure. Zeinab didn't have enough time to look after him, or the fancy old house he had bought on the Upper West Side and was so proud of. They had agreed that she would take charge of the decor and furnishings of their new house, but she couldn't even choose a color for the curtains. Zeinab had never been an expert in such things, but swore she would master the art in New York. However, she found herself unable to master anything.

She not only neglected the house; she neglected every-thing. She didn't feel she had time to even look after herself, let alone be part of Darwish's New York social life. Gradu-ally, she became isolated and depressed. She struggled to pass her exams, which made her forever anxious. She would wake up every morning feeling miserable, then waste the morning wandering around the house, doing nothing in particular. By noon, she had run out of reasons, valid or not, to procras-tinate, and finally began to study. She would struggle with topics and issues she didn't understand until five, when she'd start on dinner. And if anything ever went slightly wrong, if he made even the slightest remark on anything she'd done, she would spend the evening sulking in silent misery.

Zeinab would say that she was slow on the uptake, but not stupid. As a sensitive person, she was all too painfully aware of his dwindling respect for her. They talked about it a lot. She said she understood his reasons for it, but couldn't accept them. She tried to articulate her side of things; how she needed to feel loved and admired in order to flourish. She said she couldn't cope with his constant judging of her; his never-ending scrutiny of what she did made her confused and hesitant. She reminded him dozens of times that he had loved her despite how different they were. And she asked him hun-dreds of times why he said he loved her if he actually loathed her. He tried to explain that he understood her logic but couldn't control his anger at her many mistakes. He promised to try to curb that anger, and she promised she would make an effort to change too. But she couldn't find it in herself to even try. And he couldn't hide his annoyance. As things got worse, she threatened to leave. He laughed and asked her where she would go. When she said she'd simply vanish somewhere, he, of course, didn't believe her.

One morning, she announced she wasn't going to take the exams, or at least was going to defer them. He protested, knowing how important they were to her future, but she was adamant. She said that she wanted to focus on their life together, to get their relationship back on track. Stopping their marriage sliding was more important to her than anything else. He kept up his protests. What was she going to do, if she gave up on being a doctor? Her reply was unambiguous and determined. Yes, she was a doctor, and that was something special about her, but she couldn't risk her marriage for this. She had to regain control over her life first, then she could go back to those damned exams. Next year, or maybe the year after. He didn't agree and asked sarcastically if a housewife was all she wanted to be. She replied calmly that she'd study other things, things she'd wanted to study all her life, but hadn't had the chance to.

"Like what?" he asked wryly.

"Like the subjects you teach. Arab history, for instance."

He couldn't think of a good reply to that. He toyed with the idea of suggesting the ill-omened Hourani book, but thought better of it. Even so, she came to him a couple of days later asking if he had a good book on Arab history she could read. He got up, took the Hourani off the shelf, and gave it to her without a word.

Leila and Youssef came to live with them after their mother died. He'd always thought it was best for him and the kids to live together. Now he would be able to heal old wounds. Undo the hard knots. Reestablish relations. Their mother's death was a shock to everyone and it was felt best for the kids that they have a total change of scenery. The universities of New York could open up their minds too. New horizons.

What he didn't realize at the time was that life doesn't obey rational logic, but that everyone and everything has its own special rationale. Leila launched her war of liberation as soon as she arrived, while Youssef declared independence. Leila decided she would oust Zeinab from her father's life, saying she couldn't figure out why he'd chosen "that woman." All that New York had to offer a girl of Leila's age did nothing to appease her and, however he tried to expound Zeinab's qualities, Leila's contempt for her was unbending. Living under the same roof didn't ease her hatred of Zeinab either. It had the opposite effect, in fact. Her antipathy grew, and the tension it produced came to dominate the atmosphere in the house. It was palpable. It lay behind every little word or gesture. Who controlled the TV remote, who played their stereo and when, which lights were on or off, bedtimes, who sat where, who did their homework where, which movies they went to see, what was for dinner: it was all one remorseless battle. Leila kept trying to belittle Zeinab, and Zeinab kept trying to defend herself, to prove herself.

Youssef, meanwhile, went off to his room as soon as he arrived, and during his four years of college only emerged to eat or on his way out the door. His father kept trying to bring him out of his room, to have him sit with the rest of them, but he always failed. Whenever Darwish called him, there would be no reply. Whenever he went looking for him, he'd always find him, headphones on, plugged into his laptop. Youssef would look at him quizzically and lift one earpiece slightly. If Darwish asked him a question, the reply would be brief at best. If his father told him something, Youssef would just nod or grunt something back. Then he'd smile the same smile he used on everybody, put his headphones back on, and retreat into his world once more.

Sharing a house didn't break down any of the barriers between them. Nothing made the children happy. Leila festered in her discontent, and Youssef in his silence. And where

Darwish failed, Zeinab, of course, did too. It grieved Darwish. He wished Zeinab could magic up something to win over Youssef and Leila, but her powers as a sorceress were dismal. As much as Zeinab could tell it hurt Darwish, she sensed too that he blamed her for it in his heart. She couldn't understand that. Why blame her for everything? She could see how much his life exasperated him, and how she exasperated him even more. He made her feel a victim and a failure at the same time. They'd discuss it, argue about it, tell each other hard truths, but the wound remained painful. Each set piece just added to the despair that anything would ever change between them.

Things settled into a life perpetually on the brink. The downstairs rooms were open battlefields all the time. Arrows flew in all directions, from the kitchen and the lounge. Darwish ended up despairing at the three of them. Mimicking his son, he hid himself away in his study upstairs. He also spent more time at the university. Leila made downstairs her operations room, spending most of her time there spying on everyone's comings and goings, lunging out into the hall for a fight if she ever spotted Zeinab or Darwish.

After a few months of this, Zeinab was exhausted. She had fought on all fronts at once, without backup or allies, and without any real, obvious reason to keep on fighting. She had no desire left to prove herself to any of them: not to the angry Leila, Youssef in his own little world, or even to her withdrawn husband. And she realized Darwish had given up on her too. He didn't even deny it when she put it to him, so she lapsed into despair. She surrendered; she simply wilted. She slowly withered, and seeing her do so only made him angrier at her. He secretly blamed her for everything, including wasting away as she did.

When Leila moved to California on a master's scholarship, and Youssef to Montreal on an undergrad bursary, all that was left in the house was Darwish's silence and Zeinab's wilting. She never took her medical exams. She contemptuously rejected the very idea if he ever even mentioned it, and got mad if he pressed the point. He made a deal with an interior-design student he knew to redo the house, and used the opportunity to have the ugly curtains she had picked out for them thrown straight in the trash. He brought Kitty on to take care of the cleaning and cooking. As for Zeinab, she took to spending the day on the couch with some magazines, in front of the computer, or wandering to the shops and back, without really buying anything. She did persist with Hourani, though, reading a paragraph or two a day and taking notes, but whenever her husband came home he'd find her asleep on the couch, the book lying on her chest. He'd wake her. She'd be startled, gather up her jumble of stuff, and go straight to bed. But then one night he came home, tried to wake her up, and couldn't.

That was twenty-five years ago. Twenty-five years. He dealt with her death with a cold, steely impassivity. There were no tears. His sorrow took the form of silence and resignation, almost a continuation of his despair over her. He stayed away from women after Zeinab. It wasn't a conscious decision, but his whole being recoiled from intimacy of any kind. He didn't reflect much on Zeinab's passing back then. He avoided thinking about the meaning of her death. It wasn't necessarily because he didn't care; perhaps it was because it was more than he could bear. That was his way of dealing with it. Hiding from it. Ignoring it. Shutting himself off from it completely. He never used the word "death," but said that she had "passed on," "departed," "gone." He folded up the whole thing and put it away with the rest of his feelings.

His heart was a stopped watch. He went into deep emotional hibernation. The rest of him carried on, the part he knew and could control: his teaching, his research, his writing. He spent more time with his students, volunteered for every university committee going, supervised any thesis that came his way. The rest of his time he filled with writing and research. His reputation rose. He ended up the leading historian in his field in North America. He got numerous offers to return to Egypt and teach there. Institutions from all over the Arab world wanted him to join them, even if only for a year. He turned them all down; he saw no value in the Arabs, or in trying to teach them. In fact, he saw no point in trying to change anything or anyone anymore. He wouldn't even try. Instead, he pursued a life of being content with whatever was at hand, ambitionless for anything beyond what he could currently control. He neither relished what he had, nor pined for what he hadn't.

He even gave up on Leila and Youssef. He accepted that he could never free Leila from her anger, or Youssef from his shell. Leila completed her Master's at Berkeley, but didn't come back to New York. He made no real effort to change her mind. She worked as a lawyer in Los Angeles for several years, and had several relationships, none of which lasted. He'd ring her now and again, catch up on her news, and make the odd comment on what she was doing. The conversations would always end in barely concealed rage on her part, but that was all. A few years later, Leila went back to Egypt, wanting to "do something useful." He expressed his displeasure, but did nothing to try to prevent it. She called him a little later to say she'd met an Egyptian doctor called Luqman, whom she subsequently married and had Salma with.

She and Salma would sometimes spend the summer in New York with Darwish. Sometimes Luqman would come too. They would stay with Darwish, but not really spend time with him. It was like they happened to be guests in the same hotel. Kitty was the only one who connected them. Darwish loved Salma, but Leila prevented their relationship from developing. She kept them away from each other. He could see that, but he didn't protest. Leila cut down on those visits over time and eventually they stopped altogether. When she then broke up with Luqman, he wondered if she would then forgive him for leaving her mother. He found out later that she had started wearing the hijab and leading a more austere life back home. He had a thing or two to tell her about that over the phone, but resigned himself to it.

Youssef found a job at the UN, which took him to one African warzone after another. He never married, and Darwish never tried to persuade him to. Nor did he ever try to talk him out of his line of work, though he thought it a waste of time. When Youssef quit his job for no obvious reason, and went to live in Montreal on the pretext of writing a book, Darwish said nothing. What was the point? It wasn't that he didn't care about either of them, but he no longer tried to direct their lives. He didn't try to keep Leila in check or talk sense into Youssef. He didn't try to patch things up, resolve old differences. He had surrendered; it wasn't possible to change another person.

It was twenty-five years since he had surrendered. But what had just happened to him, slumped against his old bookcase on the floor? He clutched Hourani's book as if he had discovered a long-lost murder weapon. He saw things anew. Quietly, undramatically, he felt as if he had come to understand. As if he'd woken from a long dream. Was this how a man was supposed to discover what his life meant, sitting on the floor, browsing through his old books before dumping them in the trash? He asked himself why he hadn't seen things this way before. Twenty-five years after his wife's death, illumination had finally come from the dog-eared pages of that old book.

He saw Zeinab right there in front of him, as though she were really there. She was smiling that broad, loving smile of hers, her eyes forever imploring. That look was what he had loved most about her. He had seen it often, but it seemed he had never understood it. He saw her now and realized suddenly, acutely, how much he missed her. He longed for her as he had when he'd first met her. If she had been there at that moment, he would have asked her to marry him again.

He had wished back then that he could spend the rest of his life alone with her, and he felt the same longing now. He had thrown that all away over some ugly curtains, over spats about damned medical exams. He'd lost sight of it in all the chaos and failure of their lives together. And then, when she had died, the longing had too. But why had it come back to life? Was it because he was walking toward his own death now? Or was the iron cage into which he'd locked his heart when she died finally giving way?

He was taking a hard look at himself now. Had he committed the very sin he'd preached against every day of his life? He had taught his young students to question their prejudices and assumptions. He'd taught them to forget what they had been told and to start again. But had he ever examined his own prejudices, his own assumptions? Had he ever really taken a good look at himself? How could he have let these lofty standards and principles crush the life out of the one woman he'd really loved? Suddenly he understood why he had married her. He had loved her. It was that simple. He'd loved her, though she hadn't conformed to his ideal.

He hadn't listened to her. He realized that now. He hadn't listened, he'd just preached. Just like Jane used to say he did. Preached. What a fool he had been: a man who couldn't even hear his own wife. How stupid. He wondered if the children's bitter hostility toward her, and to him, had made him that way. There he was, trying to blame them for his own mistakes. He was to blame, for his mistakes and for theirs too. He'd sowed the seeds of unhappiness. He'd driven the two of them apart. He'd pushed the children away. Leila was brilliant, but alone and bitter. Her whole world was built on anger. She had fallen for four different boys, and then ended up marrying the fifth. Each time she would loudly declare to her father: "I've found the man I've been looking for." The man she'd been looking for. The woman he'd been looking for. Maybe she had a copy of the Hourani too. And then there was Youssef, the eternal bachelor.

Darwish was truly asking questions of himself now. How could he have presided over such chaos? Or more precisely, why could he not allow any chaos? Had he not tried to control everything, perhaps things would have turned out a little better.

He looked at his watch. Nearly seven. Youssef would be there soon. What was the point of sorting out all the books? They could go to hell. He'd phone Leila and get her to come to New York. If she turned him down again, he'd tell her he was dying and wanted to see her for the last time. If only he could go to Egypt. He wasn't up to it, though. Maybe he could get Salma to stay on; that might draw her mother over too. Maybe he could persuade her mother to get Salma into college in the US. Then maybe Leila would stay too, even if only some of the time. He'd try to convince Youssef to spend the winter in the cabin with him. He could work there on this so-called book of his. Better there than in the bitter cold of Montreal.

He'd tell them both he was sick, that he hadn't long left. Maybe they would be angry that he'd kept it quiet. They might be angry he was going to die when they had expected him to be solid and always there. This was the image that Darwish had sought to imprint on them, and encouraged them to aspire to. They would think he was deserting them, but he'd open up. He'd confess to messing up their childhoods. He wouldn't dodge it. He'd own up to his mistakes. He'd made mistakes, and was still making them. Everyone did. He'd try to be more human, maybe get them to change their mind about him. It was his last chance. Maybe the shock of it all would soften their hearts. Maybe the urgency would make them speak honestly, from the heart—let it all out. Maybe it would make them see their lives differently, face up to their errors, take some responsibility for what had happened, and learn not to repeat his mistakes. He realized, of course, that he couldn't do all this in one go, or even one visit. It would need time and perseverance. He still had a year, maybe two.

If he succeeded, it would be the greatest thing he could bequeath them. He wouldn't demand their love and devotion. He didn't dream of some happy future together. There was no future. All he hoped for was to help them leave the past behind. Maybe Leila and Youssef would spend some time at the cabin with him, even if only for a little while. And maybe when he died there, on the banks of that lake, they'd remember their last days with him, and not the past and its wounds.

Yes, that's what he would do. He'd start tonight with Youssef. He wouldn't let him hide away in his silence. And he'd phone Leila in the morning, after he'd spoken to Salma about her staying on for college. He looked at his watch again. Nearly seven. There was a lump in his throat. What was keeping Youssef? The guests were coming at eight. They wouldn't have enough time to talk. He'd have to put it off until morning, then, and speak to Leila in the afternoon. But he had to be at the lawyer's at eight thirty. He couldn't put that off. Ah, but Youssef had said he would go back to Montreal on the ten o'clock train, so they wouldn't have time to talk in the morning either. Why was he taking the train, for God's sake? Who did that? And why was he late? Hadn't he promised to come at seven and make sure the goddamn birthday party was all set up? Couldn't he turn up on time just once in his life? Just once before his old dad died? Perhaps he could take him aside during the dinner party. But that would be awkward in front of the others. No, that wouldn't work. He'd ask him to stall his travel plans tomorrow. He'd do it as soon as Youssef got there.

Yes, he'd ask him to stay on for a while. Then he could speak with him after he got back from the lawyer's. It'd all be fine. He was sure of it. All he needed to do now was get up off the floor, put Hourani back in his place, and get himself ready for Youssef and the others.

2

The Knights of Destruction

I'LL WAIT ANOTHER HOUR. THERE'S still time before Salma's party. I sip the macchiato that squats on the table in front of me. Every ten minutes that expressionless waiter peers over, like he's checking I'm still here. I know my kind doesn't belong here, but Celja wanted to meet in this place. I suggested a café in Grand Central Station. It's bigger, with perhaps less elegant clientele. And Salma's due in from DC soon. I thought I'd wait and meet her at the station, after I'd seen Celja, and go to the house with her. Salma would love that. She likes people waiting for her. But Celja said she preferred the café near her office. I didn't argue. I'll be with her for an hour at most, so no point arguing over where we meet. She said, "Let's meet at the Macchiato. Remember it?" Remember it? Of course I did. She took me there the first time. We were working at the UN building just around the block. It was in the middle of a very long day at work, and she informed me I was killing myself and deserved a little treat. She'd take me to a new place. She made me promise not to tell anyone else about it without her permission, but it only took a few weeks for all the other UN staffers to end up going there. Nothing stayed a secret for long in that place.

We're meeting at five. My train got in this afternoon and I had nothing else to do, so I went and bought some bagels on Twenty-First and came back. Dad wanted me to bring bagels. He didn't say they had to be from Montreal, though. And they wouldn't have been fresh after twelve hours on a train anyway. I remembered this shop he used to take us to when we were kids. I strolled down Twenty-First and First, got some, and walked back.

I must look such a mess. The people in this café are so well dressed. More than that, they've got that air of carefree wealth and self-possession, like they want for nothing. Spare time is scarce and they want to spend it having an espresso, a chat, some fun. Shake off work for a little while. Dump all their responsibilities for just a second. Then they run off to another meeting, get on with something else that needs doing, and spend the evening somewhere between work and pleasure. They wear dark suits, gray or black. Neckties off or, at very least, hanging down their necks a little. Pale shirts. No one checks out anyone else's clothes. They all know everyone's looking sharp. Maybe one will stop to compliment another's tie or admire the cloth of their suit, but it's pretty rare. The rule is you pretend not to notice that kind of stuff. You rise above all that, right? Once you've mastered the art, it's just a part of you. But it doesn't come without a little practice. You have to work at it if you want to come out on top. I know some of the faces here. I used to work for the same outfit. Some faces stay with you and you don't know why. Maybe we'd met in one of those endless coordination meetings, where you'd see the same people, and maybe we know a few names here and there. But it would end there.

I know these types. I was one of them myself for years. And here I am now, sitting on my own, in worn-out clothes, waiting for Celja, who's held up at HQ. With some bagels in a bag for my dad.

I called Dad to ask when Salma was getting in. He sounded pissed. I knew that tone. "Miss Salma missed her train and won't get in before midnight."

"Midnight? Why bother with a birthday party at all then?"

He replied irritably, "It's a dinner, not a birthday party."

Then he wondered oh-so-drily if I was expecting balloons and party hats, before telling me to get there no later than seven.

At five fifteen, my cell phone rings. It's Celja.

"I called you a half hour ago, but your phone was out. Where are you?"

"The Macchiato, like you said."

"Sorry, I'm running late. Incident in Darfur. I have to stay on an hour till I finish the statement."

"What kind of incident?"

"The usual."

"Where?"

"El-Fasher."

"Big?"

"No. Just the usual. No clear details yet. About five dead, though."

"About?"

"Yeah. Conflicting reports."

"What do our people on the ground say?"

"Different numbers from each office. You know how it works. But the secretary-general's office wants the exact figure before deciding on the wording."

"Do you know how long it's going to take?"

"Hour. Hour and a quarter. No longer. It's the usual stuff. I'll just make sure on the number so I can get the wording right. I'll pass the draft on from the director and the mission in Khartoum, and up to the twenty-eighth floor."

"I'll wait, but remember I have dinner at my dad's at seven."

"You can't hang on an hour or two?"

"Are you kidding? Do you remember my dad at all?"

"I'll do what I can, and let you know how it goes."

"I'll hang on."

"I'll hang on" is what I had said to the head of mission too. "I'll hang on for the night here and come back tomorrow." He praised my initiative to begin with, because a day had not been long enough to deal with the problem. He had to catch a plane to Khartoum before sundown, because the regulations on using helicopters made that the only other option out of there. I'd spend the night and then speak to the three refugees who had agreed to be witnesses about what had happened at the camp. I'd authenticate their statements, then speak to the camp authorities to ensure their safety after I left. I'd get a plane in the morning. But my boss objected: "You don't have a security pass from the mission to stay overnight in the camp. Staffers aren't allowed to stay overnight without permission. Insurance reasons."

"Insurance reasons?"

"Yes, that's right. It's the latest thing security and HR have come up with."

We talked it over and ended up agreeing we'd pretend we didn't know anything about this latest batch of red tape. One of us had to stay to finish the task we'd been charged with. We'd talked for months about the violations at the camp, and the attacks on refugees happening right in front of the authorities' eyes. They always denied it, of course, saying there was no evidence. Relief workers and doctors had documented rapes, broken bones, amputated limbs. It was all no use, though, because the survivors were too scared to testify anyway.

Our planes, landing in the red mud, were surrounded by dozens of children utterly unfazed by the enveloping dust clouds. We were welcomed as saviors, then loaded into huge SUVs that kicked up new dust clouds behind them as they set off. We rattled over the rocky dirt roads and raced straight over to the camp. We walked past the rows of tin shacks, which had for years housed the refugees who hoped to return to their villages one day. Every pair of eyes was fixed on our convoy. We drove on into the heart of the camp and the official reception committee. The officials tried in every way they could to waste our time, insisting we eat with them first. When we politely declined, they protested that we would offend local custom if we didn't. That's where I came in. I spoke to them in Egyptian Arabic, and they soon realized their delaying tactics dressed as phony cultural sensitivity were exposed, so they moved on to other ruses. After half an hour of further dodging, we finally got them around to the reason we'd come: to talk to the refugees. We sat under a tree and the refugees gathered around us, all talking at the same time. Over and over, they yelled their demands at us, which we knew anyway. Complaints about camp conditions. Demands for protection. We asked them about violations and they said they happened daily. We asked them who usually carried out the attacks and they told us it was the Janjaweed militias. They said they were everywhere, among those who worked at the camp, disguised as refugees and even relief workers. I translated all of this for my boss but our patience was wearing thin. We needed precise details: specific, consistent, and credible statements that could substantiate the accusations. We needed them to speak our language, but they weren't going to do that. That is, until I talked to two young men in their twenties and a fifteen-year-old girl. They said they would talk specifics and name names. They said they could identify the perpetrators and would give statements. I summoned the camp's chief warden, and told him he was personally responsible for the safety of those three. I decided to stay and see the task through. I wasn't going to let this one slip by.

Celja had called me: "Youssef, where are you?"

"El-Fasher."

"What? Why? Haven't you left yet?"

"I'm staying overnight. The boss is going back with the team. I've got some work I've got to finish up here. I'll come back tomorrow. Are you in the office?"

"Yes."

"Don't stay too late."

That was the first time I spent the night in Darfur. I usually worked in Khartoum or outside of the country: Addis Ababa, Nairobi, N'Djamena, Abuja, New York. I rarely went to Darfur at all, even though it was my area of responsibility.

The camp changed after my boss left. The clamor died down and the refugees went back to their shelters. The relief workers dispersed, most of them leaving the camp to go back to their offices. The camp authorities took control again. I walked around the camp with Enrico, one of the relief workers, accompanied by camp officials as always, "to protect us." Then I sat alone with the three witnesses. The two young men talked at length about the attacks on them. They were from different tribes, but they had both studied law for two years at Khartoum University. But then they started mixing their studies with militia activities. They told me different, but similar tales about their lives in their villages. The men on horseback would come and attack them, burn down the villagers' huts, kill the livestock, and drop some of the carcasses down the wells in order to poison them. They killed whomever of the men they wanted to, and dismembered those they didn't kill and who hadn't run away. When the male villagers had all been dealt with, they would rape the women in front of those who remained, then charge off in a dust storm back to where they had come from. The two young men both said that any remaining villagers would flee their homes the same night on foot, carrying what they could, until they got to the camp. People from other villages told them that the attackers would come back repeatedly to the same villages to make a further example of those who had stayed. None of this was new to me, as I'd heard such stories many times before. I asked about conditions in the camp, and how attacks had happened there when the authorities and security staff were present.

Now the girl spoke, encouraged by the other two. She spoke clearly and assuredly, looking me directly in the eye. She said she and other girls collected firewood every day and the guards and wardens always harassed them as they did it. Persecution was routine. The problem was the sporadic Janjaweed attacks on the camp, and that there were people in the camp who gave the Janjaweed information. She gave the names, tribal affiliations, and job titles of these informers. The chief warden, whom she called a complete incompetent with no idea what was going on around him, was not one of their number, but there were those who worked directly under him who had direct links to the security forces "who threaten us." I asked why they had threatened them, and she replied that the government was trying to force them out of the camp and into other villages they had set up far away from their own, hundreds of miles from their lands. The government was clearing them off their land in order to hand it over to the very tribes that had attacked those in the camp. She said that anyone who refused to move out was subjected to these attacks. I asked if her people had been asked to move. She nodded, and said they had refused. I asked if they had been threatened and she said they had. I asked if there had been a follow-up on that threat and she said without flinching that she, her mother, and her sister had been raped.

The waiter picks up my macchiato cup and asks me if I want anything else. I thank him and ask for another, plus a mineral water. He nods, clears my table, and walks off. The small white tables are close together. The chairs are just stools really, maybe to encourage the clientele not to hang around for too long. Most of the tables are raised, without chairs around them; just customers hurriedly gulping down their coffees while standing around, swapping stories, updating one another, leaking information to one another, then heading out. No one has sat here as long as I have. For God's sake, Celja! None of the others customers look at me. They brush past me, borrow chairs for their table from mine, step around me to talk nearby in private. Not the slightest glance is wasted on me, as though I'm part of the furniture. Have I really left this all behind? I had never thought I would. Do I really want to step back into their shoes so I can proclaim how utterly weary I am of my work, while really being utterly convinced of my own importance? Certainly my work had been vital, though I would deny this out of false modesty. I've always believed that modesty is not really an expression of humility. It's rampant vanity. Modesty is for the exalted who graciously descend to consort with the lower orders, so as to inflate their own sense of self-importance. It's certainly not about lowering yourself to the level of others. To be humble you have to be sure that you are, in fact, quite superior.

I was ever so humble back then. I can't do it anymore. No regular job. Living off my savings in my rundown place in Montreal, pretending to do research for a book. An imaginary book. I have nothing to be modest about anymore. Yet this is the course I chose the day I found out that what power I thought I had was an illusion. What I thought was my ability to influence was as insubstantial as a ghost. What remained of me now to hold on to? It seemed I was a creature not worthy of even a glance from those who were just like I once was.

My cell phone rings: Celja again.

"Yes?"

"Don't be angry, but I'm still waiting."

"You still don't know how many were killed?"

"No, it's not that. What we still don't know is if there were any militiamen killed."

"Militiamen? Wasn't it in a refugee camp? Have the refugees got guns as well nowadays?"

"This is no joke, Youssef. A lot has happened since you left, including rebel movements now operating in the camps, believe it or not. The government reports say it's not attacks from the outside, but clashes breaking out inside. The tone of the statement might have to be very different."

"Well, obviously some things haven't changed at all. OK. Do you know how much longer it'll be?"

"I don't know; maybe a half hour. When are you leaving?"

"Tomorrow morning."

"I've got to see you before you disappear again. Couldn't you put off traveling tomorrow?"

"I've got stuff to do in Montreal."

"But tomorrow we'll have more time to talk, rather than snatching a few minutes together tonight."

"Well, there could be something else tomorrow. Congo, Somalia, whatever."

"OK, so why not come to the office? All I'm doing is sitting around waiting. We could talk."

"Come on, Celja. You know I'll never set foot in there again."

"OK, OK, I'll do what I can, but don't leave without telling me."

"OK."

My cell phone beeps, I'll be out of juice soon. Great. How come it's so hard for me to remember to charge it overnight? Of course, I don't know where the charger is. It could be in my bag, or I could have left it at home or somewhere else.

My interview with the two young men and the girl ended after nearly two hours. The girl had spoken in the most brutal detail about what had happened to her mother, her sister, and herself. Her tone did not fluctuate once during the whole time she spoke. It neither rose nor fell. No sighing, no faltering, no breaking off, as people often do when they tell such stories. It was as if she were narrating for an audiobook. I knew she was genuine. No one could manufacture that kind of demeanor. It was the manner of someone who had completely detached herself from her emotions in order to keep a grip, so as not to crumble. It was the manner of someone who had survived hell.

Relief workers, to some extent, experience terrible things too, without realizing their impact. They travel from one tragedy to another, thinking themselves immune. Then they suddenly crumble. We say they've burned out. Like lightbulbs.

The girl said that she knew who the three rapists were, and that they were all camp security guards. They'd even seen them afterward, more than once. They had made obscene gestures at them, reminders of what they had done. I asked about her father and brothers. She said she didn't know where her brothers were. Maybe they were dead, or maybe in another camp somewhere. Her father knew what had been done to them, but had been powerless to do anything. He couldn't leave the camp to confront the guards. And he still sent her and her sister out collecting firewood, despite what had happened. She said she was prepared to undergo a medical exam, testify before a judge, and give detailed evidence that could identify and condemn the perpetrators. This was exactly what I had been looking for. I praised her for her courage and promised her protection. We agreed that we would go with Enrico to the directorate in the morning to make a statement. Then I'd fly back to Khartoum. I contacted Celja and asked her to inform the chief of mission, then went to bed in one of the small rooms attached to our camp offices. The camp chief offered me a bed in the government lodge, but I refused. I also refused Enrico's offer of a bed in the UN lodge, so he decided to bunk with me in solidarity.

It must have been close to nine when I heard a sound I would never forget. It came from the belly of the earth, like a regular pounding on a giant drum hidden beneath the earth's crust, shaking our feet with its vibrations. My gaze met Enrico's. Was this what I thought it was? He nodded. I ran toward the door, I don't know why, but he pulled me back onto the bed.

"Don't do anything crazy. Sit down."

"Is it the Janjaweed?"

"Has to be."

"How do they have the nerve to come while we're here?"

"Nerve's something they're not short of. Keep quiet. Not a sound."

"What should we do?"

"Nothing. We keep quiet and stay here. They probably won't attack our offices."

"Probably? What's going to happen out there?"

"They'll attack some of them. Pray to God it's no worse than usual."

"Pray? Is that all we can do? Can't we contact anyone?"

"Of course we can, but there's no need. Word travels fast. The whole country will know by now."

"And the security forces?"

"They'll come. But only when the Janjaweed have gone."

"Well, what if we go out there now? They surely won't attack UN people? We can protect the refugees."

"Have you gone mad? Go out and defend forty thousand civilians? You and me? Be quiet and sit here till they've gone. These things happen all the time. There are rules to them. Your life will be in danger if you go out there."

I looked for my cell phone. Thank God it still had some charge. I called the head of mission. No reply. I called Celja and told her what was happening. I asked her to tell the chief of mission straightaway. She asked me to keep my head and not do anything stupid. Enrico told me to mute my phone, so I did, and then sat there waiting. Nothing. Sitting there in that narrow little room, in a dark suit, with a satellite phone, with Enrico the veteran. We listened to the pounding hooves dispersing the refugees. There were no screams, just this pounding coming from the belly of the earth, crashing and grunting. Nothing else. My phone lit up. The chief of mission, checking we were all OK. He said he'd contacted the highest authorities he could reach and they had promised to intervene straightaway. I thanked him and hung up. We sat in silence for another hour, locked away in our little room with the knights of destruction outside the door.

Enrico looked at his phone. He said the Janjaweed had gone. He'd received a message from outside the camp confirming they'd seen them go. We rushed outside. It was all quiet. Not a sound, nothing moved. Then, after a few minutes, there were stirrings. People came to see what damage had been done.

Then came the lamentations. Five dead: two young men, two young women, and one of the guards. People gathered in large groups, consumed with rage, smashing anything in their reach. A few minutes later the guards came out, exacerbating the anger of the crowds. It wasn't long before there was a confrontation between the refugees and the guards surrounding the camp. I was told someone else was killed. I saw Enrico trying to mediate between the two sides. I wandered around, not knowing what I was looking for. I couldn't believe this was happening around me, and that I was so useless. Everyone there knew it. None of them came to me for help, or even to speak to me. I went along with the crowd, not knowing where we were heading. The security guards had withdrawn from the camp, patrolling the outskirts until relief workers could take over negotiations between the authorities and the refugees.

I marched along with a crowd of people and then stopped. I heard prayers to God and lamentations once again: "There is no might or power except in God." I saw the two corpses, like the remains of a burnt-out car, charred flesh melded with scorched clothes. Voices rose, then men appeared with sheets to gather up the charred remains lying in front of us. They wrapped them up as if they were whole corpses and the gathering, myself included, carried the bodies away. Then I felt a strong arm dragging me away from the middle of the crowd. I looked around to see Enrico that had me in a steely grip. I didn't put up a fight. He took me back to the office and locked the door on me, and I sat there motionless until he returned. I don't know long it was before he came back. He told me it was an hour. He shook his head with a mixture of impatience and despair. I learned that the bodies were the girl I had spoken to yesterday and her sister, rape victim number two. The Janjaweed had set fire to them, stood watching them burn, then left, bragging about it. Enrico told me that one of them had taken a photo of their burning bodies on his phone. The two boys I had spoken to that day were also among the dead. The guard, it appeared, had dared to intervene to try and rescue the girls, and had been shot dead by one of the raiders on horseback.

My phone vibrated next to me. I did not move. Enrico picked it up and I heard him speak first to Celja, then to the head of mission. He repeated to them what he'd told me, and added that he'd seen a picture of the girl on fire. There were no pictures of the attackers' faces in the shot. They were masked anyway. Silence; then he went on to say that this had been a bad idea, as was the idea that any of the refugees would testify against their assailants. Silence again, then he added: "Of course this isn't the first time." He added that I was OK, and asked her to phone back in an hour.

She's calling again.

"I'm almost done. I've got all the details. I've made it clear that there were four killed, all unarmed. I've written two versions of a statement, one 'condemning,' one 'regretting.' I've sent them both to the director. Waiting to hear back. I usually send both versions to the secretary general's office as soon as he gives me permission. He doesn't interfere in the format, but insists on seeing everything I send up to the twenty-eighth floor. I'll wait for the office to reply. Then I'll put the statement into its final form and send it to the official spokesman. A half hour more at most. Aren't you happy you're done with all this?"

"Very happy. Don't be upset, though, if we don't manage to catch up. We'll meet up next time."

"Next time? Are you joking? You haven't been to New York since Christmas. Where have you come from, anyway?"

"Montreal."

"Montreal? By train?"

"Yeah. And going back by train too."

"Still not catching planes? How long did that take? You must be exhausted. God, I'm so sorry!"

"Don't apologize. Just let me see you before I catch the next train."

"Can't you stay in the city one more night?"

"Celja!"

"Right, right. I'll be with you as soon as the secretary general decides whether to condemn or regret."

"I'll be sitting right here."

My phone's battery is on its last bar of charge. If only she'd stop calling every ten minutes. It won't last much longer, but I can't tell her that. She'd have gotten annoyed. I'll wait. What else can I have to do before Dad's dinner party, anyway? As long as I'm not late. He expects me to be late, just to prove to him again how disorganized and useless I am; that his son's a joke. Nobody's organized compared to him, of course. I don't see the point of being so programmed and precise. He's like a soldier ant with iron discipline, moving in his unchanging patterns, waiting for someone to come along and crush him underfoot. He always wants us on time, even if the world is going to end tomorrow. I'll bet if he knew when he was going to die, he'd turn up to face his destiny on the dot. There was no point talking to him about all of this. I've tried often enough, and all he does is lambast me with his logic and flaunt his parental authority. I don't want to have to scream back in his face that what he feels is all a delusion. Real things happen without regularity, logic, or rationale. Like death. Like injustice. Like impotence.

Leila didn't back down like I had. She fought back to the end. It ended with her leaving America behind and going back to Egypt. She hadn't come out well from all this; none of us had. And now there's Salma. No doubt he wants to rescue her from the clutches of "her crazy mother." But who really knew what was going on with the girl or her mother? He barely knew Salma's age, yet he wanted to save her all the same. He wanted her to finish her studies in America and settle down there, just like he had wanted us to do.

Salma asks me what she should do. She's talked to me every day on the phone since she arrived. She's showered me with questions: about her grandfather, her father, her mother;

about my aunt Amira and her husband Daoud, who also lived in the US; about anything else you could imagine.

"You're my uncle," she says. "You've spent most of your life here, but you know Egypt too, and you've traveled to tons of places. You've experienced lots of things."

She says all this as if she were reciting it from a book. She asks me questions and I've got no answers. What can I tell her about life here, or life there, about the crucial choices in life that can change everything or make no difference at all? What can I offer except a few hackneyed observations about people and their vileness wherever they are from, about useless hopes and prayers unanswered? I have nothing to tell her. I listen to her. I stammer a few banalities. I point her in her mother's direction, or her father's. Then, when all else fails, I act like all the shrinks I've seen: I ask her how she feels, and how she sees it, and then leave her to it.

A guy comes over and asks if he can leave his jacket on the chair opposite me. I nod. The place is full and the chair's been empty for a while. Come on, Celja. Get the secretary general to either condemn or regret! If only I had insisted on another café. I could have eaten something at least. I could have avoided being among these high-flying types, bringing back all these memories. I wonder whether, deep down, I miss this world. The corridors of HQ oozed a sense of power, but there was no real power there. Power came from the capitals of the world to wander its legendary corridors, walk down its passageways, sometimes almost colliding. You imagine you are at the center of power, but you're just a pebble in the stream. You could spend your whole life not knowing the truth of it. And you could, as I did, wake up suddenly to the delusion of it all and refuse to spend the rest of your life being carried along in the current. You leap clear. So what, then, makes me wonder if I miss those corridors?

*

Celja phoned back and Enrico passed the phone to me. I told her I was OK. I answered a few questions earnestly. She then passed the phone to the head of mission. He said many things about sorrow and regret.

"I'm fine," I said. "Nothing at all happened to me. But those we spoke to yesterday—all killed. All of them."

He repeated his regrets, and said the incident would not be allowed to pass.

I asked, "What will you do about it? How will you not let it pass?"

He said he'd spoken to New York, and the Security Council would meet that night to issue a statement he expected to be very strongly worded. I asked him angrily how some statement would deal with the tragedy that had just taken place, and that would take place again and again. He asked me what I wanted him to do—send in UN forces to the camp? I said his sarcasm was inappropriate and asked, if he really couldn't protect these people, why he had deluded us into thinking he could. He said some ugly stuff about the realities of life and I exploded back at him that the whole thing was contemptible, and that the blood of those killed that night was on his hands. His. Personally. He said I was getting overwrought, and handed the phone back to Celja. She asked me to calm down, and said she'd send a helicopter for me at first light. I hung up. Enrico said he had to go out again, as there was work he needed to finish. He asked me if I could last an hour without doing anything else stupid. I nodded.

He went outside and, a few moments later, I did too, to wander around the camp. Enrico would be angry, but so what? I couldn't stay in that room. While the door was shut, I thought I heard the muffled thumping on the ground return. I went out for a walk, not wanting to do any harm. After a while, I found myself drinking tea with a group of young men in front of one of the shelters. An hour after that I was in the camp canteen. A guy who it seemed I had once smoked shisha with came over and gave me his cell phone.

I looked at the screen, and at first couldn't work out what I was looking at. A lamp or something like that was flickering like a dancer. By the time I understood what it was, it was too late. Ablaze, she had run into the middle of a circle. Whenever she ran to one edge of the circle one of the men on horseback shoved her back in with a stick. The flames burning her flickered irregularly, perhaps with the wind. After a few minutes, her movements slowed. She stood in the middle of the ring, then stumbled forward a step or two until she was pushed back into the middle. She stood still, and the flames settled and then gradually subsided. Suddenly she jerked about as if she were sitting down and trying to stand up, but couldn't do it. She remained like that, seeming to half move as the fire died down, leaving a thin plume of smoke trailing from her. All this chaos, and the authorities still doubted there were militia members in the camp.

At around midnight Celja called again to go over the sequence of events and the precise wording of the statements. She said the government report claimed that it was the girls' own family that had set fire to them to put a stop to their immoral conduct, and that camp security had tried to intervene to save them. The guards, it said, had fired warning shots in self-defense when crowds of refugees had attacked them, leading to chaotic scenes in which one of the soldiers and two youths were killed. The authorities said that they suspected armed elements in the camp had orchestrated it all.

I screamed at Celja, maybe for the first time in my life. She was extremely upset and asked me to give the phone to Enrico. She phoned an hour later to say that they would not accept the government report, based on the statements of the relief workers, but they would soften the tone of their statement. There had been a strong exchange of views in the Security Council between those who insisted on a condemnation of the government for failing to protect the refugees, and those who simply wanted to express regret at the incident.

After I hung up on her, the cell-phone battery died altogether. I threw the phone on the bed and lay there until morning, when the UN security team arrived and escorted me to the plane that took me back to Khartoum.

It's six thirty. I need to go now to get there on time, otherwise I'll get that look from Dad that I so loathe. I look at the bag of bagels. Hasn't he figured out yet that I've been out of work for two years? Did he switch off after his desire to see me become an important person was realized, after all the effort and money he had put into my education? He wanted me to be a lawyer, but I refused. I dashed his hopes back then, but he seemed to find some solace in my joining the UN. Thank God he stopped scrutinizing the details of my life after that. I never told him I was burned out, and could no longer look my bosses and colleagues in the eye; I couldn't face the building itself, or even getting on a plane. I told him I was writing a book in the peace and quiet of my Montreal home.

He asked me a few questions at the time, and then fell into a skeptical silence. He'll be happy when he sees the bagels. Not that he was likely to actually eat any of them. But he'll be happy just because I remembered. He was testing me, like he always does. Like insisting I arrive at the house at seven, to supervise the preparations for Salma's birthday party. What exactly would I supervise? Would Professor Darwish really leave important matters like arranging a dinner party in my hands? Of course not. Kitty would sort everything out, with him personally overseeing her. It was just an experiment to see if I was really a good boy, if I honored my commitments, as if I were still a kid that needed rearing. God help you, Salma, if you're staying.

My cell phone rings: Celja again. I press the green button, but the battery dies before she can say anything. There isn't much time left anyway. I'll wait ten more minutes. Maybe she'll show up. And then I'll go to the dinner party.

3

Turning to Mark

Rami quickly straightened his collar when he saw the conductor open the carriage door. He was always worried that his undershirt was showing. He tugged his jacket collar over it to make sure it wasn't. The conductor passed by without looking at him, even though he'd been sitting there for two hours. However, he did stop at the young woman who had boarded at the last stop. He checked her ticket and headed back to the dining car. The train was full; people heading for New York for the weekend. It was peak time and he'd paid a whole 122 dollars. If he'd waited until the morning after to travel, it would have saved him forty dollars, but he would have missed Professor Darwish's dinner, and it was the first time Professor Darwish had invited him to his house in years. Rami had bought the more expensive ticket, but ended up missing the train like an idiot because he'd fallen asleep in Washington. He couldn't believe he'd done that, but he had been exhausted after twenty-two hours on the train from Miami. He had no idea how he'd been able to sleep on the marble floors of Union Station, but he had. He woke to realize his train had gone, and with it any chance of making his dinner date, or anything else he had arranged for that matter. He was on the point of giving up on it all, but made a dash instead for the last train to New York. He didn't know exactly what he would do when he got there; he'd have to work that out along the way.

It would take about another hour and a half to reach New York. The girl in his train car must be going there too. She looked only a bit older than his daughter Sasha. She had put her headphones on as soon as she sat down, but kept the music low. She leaned over and asked him if the noise bothered him, but he told her it didn't. Nice girl. Well, seemed to be, but who could really tell? Maybe she had stolen money off her parents.

He patted the fourteen dollars in his pocket and smiled wryly to himself. He no longer bore a grudge. What had happened had happened, and things were how they were. He bore no grudge toward anyone: neither his boss, nor his wife, nor either of his daughters. They had all behaved as their characters had dictated. There was nothing surprising in this, so what was the use in being sour about it? It still made him feel sad, though. He hadn't expected all of this acrimony. He was angry at himself and reflected that, if he had brought up his daughters better, if he had been less easygoing in the way he'd raised them, they might have treated him better. He had thought about that a whole lot over the last few months. Yet every time he did, he came to the same conclusion: the time to worry about it all was long gone.

He wondered what Salma was like now. Was she like his daughters, or had her Egyptian upbringing made her turn out differently? He hadn't seen her since she was ten, and girls change quickly at that age. Incredibly quickly. He looked at his watch and then his ticket. He would be in New York around midnight. He'd go straight to Darwish's house, where Mark would pick him up and take him to stay with him in Brooklyn. Once he'd settled in at Mark's, he would think all these things through properly.

Rami, sitting in that train compartment, fourteen dollars in his pocket, hadn't always been in such dire straits. He'd been head of his household, with two teenage daughters and a well-paid job in a big PR firm that had paid off the mortgage on his big Miami house. He'd led a sober, steady kind of life. He'd gotten on with neighbors and colleagues. He had never been someone who particularly stood out and had never aroused any great interest, one way or the other, from any of those neighbors and colleagues. He wasn't the type you'd invite over for dinner to show off to your other guests, but he was well respected, reliable, quiet, friendly, and conservative in his habits and morals. He accepted difference and never stuck his nose in other people's affairs.

He went to university in New York and graduated from the Middle Eastern Studies Department, and then worked on a three-year research project with Professor Darwish. Darwish liked him, not just because he was a distant relation—Rami's cousin was married to one of Darwish's—but because he was a good-hearted type and straight with everyone. Rami was hardworking too: an important quality in a researcher. Darwish saw a promising future for him if he stayed in academia, but then a high-flying job in a top PR and marketing firm made Rami change tack. The monthly pay was more than a year's salary at the university, even with a professorship. So he accepted the position. That didn't exactly please Darwish. He was dismayed Rami would even think about taking it, livid he'd thrown away the opportunity he'd given him. He liked and respected Rami, but felt he had conferred a substantial honor on him by letting him work on his team, only for Rami to be bought off with a handful of dollar bills. How cheap! Angrily, Darwish let him leave, and once a year Rami would get in touch to find out how he was, but always got the same curt response. Darwish never initiated contact, but he allowed Rami to keep in touch and would invite him over when he was in New York. There Rami met Salma, the professor's granddaughter. Salma was a sweet kid who always tried to befriend those she didn't know, and wasn't afraid of strangers. When Rami visited his old teacher in the summertime, Salma was usually there, vacationing with her mother in the city. Sometimes he would bring Sasha with him, and they would all go out together, to the movies or for a picnic. But all that was done with now. These last few years he had rarely gone to New York, and Professor Darwish didn't invite him around anymore when he did. Their communication dwindled to cards sent by Rami in the holiday seasons and Darwish's terse responses. That was why Rami was so knocked out to be invited over for dinner. Of course he had eagerly accepted, even if it would cost him the last dollar in his pocket to get there.

Ever since he had moved to Miami to work for the PR firm, life had been good, steady. His wife, Maria, who was born in Cuba to a Lebanese family, taught Spanish in a private school near his house. Their two daughters were doing well in school, and seemed likely to get into an Ivy League university. The one thing that always nagged away at Rami was his sense of loneliness. He could never explain it to anyone, and even when he did try to express to Maria what he meant by it, it always ended in a quarrel. He turned to Sasha, who was older and wiser than his youngest, Marta. He tried to explain, but words failed him. He, a translator no less, couldn't find the words in English to express exactly what he meant. This weighed on him even more. It struck him that this was the very definition of loneliness: trying to explain something to your own daughter in a language that was not your own, knowing you would never be understood in your mother tongue. He went quiet that day and then changed the subject. Sasha, however, was going through that phase in which young girls try to act the adult and engage with their parents' grown-up conversations. She wanted to break out of being the typical teenager, only talking about herself and listening to no one else, so she kept at him until he began to talk. He started by telling her that he felt alone in the sense that he'd had to rely only on himself to get by for his entire life. She replied that that was how America was for everyone. He agreed, but reminded her that this wasn't the only world he knew. There was another that he could still remember: "A world of family and friends who help you out when times are tough. You know they're always there, and they'll stand by you whenever you need them. Emotionally, financially, whatever."

He told her stories about his family in Egypt, all the holidays they had been on when he was a child, the relationships he'd had with relatives, friends, and neighbors. Every year he'd go back and things were just as they had been: everything was reassuringly familiar, as if he'd only left the day before. Sasha's response to this was that people always exaggerated the charms of the past, but he shook his head sorrowfully. He told her he'd never made any real friends in America, even though he'd lived most of his life there. Not in the way he had in Egypt. Some might put his lack of American friends down to a lack of free time, but he believed it was the American way of life itself, full stop. He asked her if she could just drop in on her friends without phoning first, and explained how absurd it would seem in Egypt to have to do that. A friend over there knew they could drop in on you anytime.

Rami kept talking and Sasha kept listening, cutting in with questions from time to time. The more she asked, the more open he became with her. In the end, he admitted that he felt alone talking to his own wife and daughters in a language that wasn't his own. He knew he couldn't really watch Egyptian movies starring Shadia, Suad Hosni, or Magda with them. They couldn't really listen to the great Abdel-Halim Hafez together. He knew he'd have to translate everything, as if he were still at work. A translator by night as well as by day, having to translate not just words, but whole concepts. He had to explain what he meant every time he spoke of the things he loved and hated, or when he told them about things that had happened in Egypt or were happening there now. Loneliness was to be stuck in one place while those who loved you were in another. It was an abyss he had to try to span every time he spoke.

Rami hadn't planned to tell his daughter all this; he hadn't even realized that was how he felt. But when she asked her questions he replied, and the confidence and warmth he sensed from her made him open up, let it all out. Telling his clever elder daughter all this, Rami had no idea it would spark off a chain reaction that would unravel his whole life.

Rami didn't plummet; he gradually slid. It was a whole chain of events that didn't really have to go the way it did. In fact, some of the events seemed random and disconnected at the time, but that's how these things work sometimes. Not all our choices inevitably follow on from events. Sometimes, torn between two choices, we end up taking one without much thought, only to find ourselves obliged to make another choice afterward, only to find another fork ahead. And so it goes on. And then, maybe a year later, we find ourselves in a landscape we'd never dreamed of inhabiting. Sometimes we can trace our steps back, but most times we can't, so we just press ahead. At other times, we fix on one direction to take, and give up everything that might stand in our way, against the advice and warnings of friends. We say to ourselves that this is the price we must pay to remain true to ourselves, to realize our potential or to achieve this or that. And twenty years later we look back and don't even remember what sent us down that road in the first place.

The road to Rami's ruin was like that. It was a series of choices he'd spent little time mulling over, one leading to the next and, eventually, to the wreck of the life he had built for himself over thirty years. He told Sasha his innermost secrets. He confessed to the estrangement he'd felt ever since he'd landed in America. And that confession had had two direct consequences.

The first was that Sasha was shocked by her father's confession; it confirmed what she had long suspected in her heart. Her father didn't really love them at all. He'd just wound up having to share his life with them. He'd just gone along with it all. She, her sister, and her mother were on one side and her father—silent, with nothing to say—was on the other.

It confirmed what she had long suspected, but never dared to admit, not even to herself: her father was not like them. The three of them were normal, natural, engaged in the life they found around them. He had been an awkward, alien presence in their lives from their early schooldays until now, especially when they had friends over. Their mother was beautiful and powerful, though admittedly a bit brash along with it, but she always welcomed her classmates into their home. She showered them with attention and questions, as well as food, and their families liked her a lot. Sure, her sister was crazy, but no more so than other girls her age. He was the strange element in their world—the Arab immigrant who had never adapted. Sasha had no time for that immigrant mentality. They leave their country for a new life in another, then complain about being in exile. She now realized that she always felt, secretly, that her father was dragging her away from the normal life she wanted. Now it seemed he wanted to pull them all even further apart. She did not exactly articulate this in her head as such, but the sense of it stalked her heart. Then she asked herself the obvious question: "Where is he going with all this? Where does he want this to take us?"

The second consequence was for Rami. He now fully recognized what he had felt deep down for years and hadn't been able to put into words, or even clearly formulate in his head. Now that he had, he was surprised by the distance between where he was now and where he had wanted to be. He was shocked to realize his life had gone down a road he hadn't wished it to take; one that had annihilated every ambition he'd once had. He asked himself why he hadn't thought this through before, but he'd been busy building a life, chasing stability, professional advancement, and financial security for himself and his family. Above all, he'd looked after his wife and his daughters, his children's upbringing and education, the house, and what was left of his family in Egypt. This had been the greater, more pressing concern in his daily life, and it hadn't left him much time to ponder ideas of isolation. Now, with the children approaching college age, the evidence of his solitude engulfed him. At first he told himself it was just the kind of bereavement all fathers feel when their children leave home. He tried to tell his wife all this but failed. He tried to find a true friend to confide in but, when he realized he really had none in America, he finally grasped that the problem was much deeper than he'd thought.

Sasha had encouraged him to express his true feelings, with her tender questioning, but from that time on, his sense of loneliness and his resentment at being its prisoner grew and grew. And the more he reflected on these feelings, the more they preoccupied him, until he could think of nothing else.

His confession to Sasha and its two consequences produced a third consequence in his wife, Maria. Sasha's anxiety at her father's confession to such lugubrious thoughts was overwhelming. As she couldn't resolve in her own mind what was behind her father's confession, or what to do about it, she decided to share it with her sister Marta, who was younger than her, and not quite so smart. Marta, whom everyone saw as the hysterical one in the family, panicked. She yelled back at her sister that this meant their father wanted to take them away from America and back to Egypt for sure. Sasha dismissed it as crazy talk from her crazy little sister, but Marta kept at her. Two things backed up what Marta was saying, and she explained them both for Sasha's benefit. First, their dad was fifty-seven. He had nothing left to strive for in America. Second, he'd felt lonely at the thought of them leaving home. That was natural. Decades of routine married life had snuffed out any spark in his relationship with their mother. That was natural too. So how does he deal with it? Marta asked the question, then answered it herself without waiting for her sister.

"Normal people cheat on their wives, hook up with someone else. But these immigrant weirdos like Dad start pining for the old country."

Sasha was unconvinced. This wasn't the first time Marta had come out with bizarre theories, even about the most ordinary things. Then Marta reminded her of what had happened to Myrna and Laura two years before, and of Huda, who had run away from home when her father had tried to force her to go to Syria, and other stories like that. They always followed the same old logic: "They all panic when their girls get to 'marrying age,' and suddenly want to go back home."

But Sasha was still unconvinced by the case Marta made.

It could have all ended there if crazy Marta had not run to her shrewd mother to warn her of the impending catastrophe, and if Sasha herself had not begun to have her doubts, even if she didn't fully accept Marta's theory. It could have even ended there if Rami himself had not demonstrated a sudden urge to take Maria and the girls off to Egypt for the three months of summer. That really made Maria anxious. They had never spent more than two consecutive weeks there before. Maria, who often described her mixed heritage as part practical American girl, part bolshie Cubana, and part savvy Lebanese, decided to take control. Six months after that, to the day, she divorced Rami. He lost everything, even the children wouldn't see him.

Rami didn't want to be late for Darwish, because the professor was a stickler for punctuality. Rami had no cell phone to tell him he couldn't make it either. A cell phone was one of the many things he'd had to get used to living without over the last three months. He'd get to New York at midnight, but then what? The dinner party would be over. He wouldn't see Salma. Mark would be at Professor Darwish's precisely at midnight, so he had to get there by then. He checked the ticket for an arrival time, and checked too for any screens onboard to work out what time they were making, but couldn't see any. He realized that if he wanted to know what time the train got in he'd have to ask. He thought about asking the young girl to his left, but thought better of it. She probably wouldn't know anyway. He figured he'd ask the conductor when he came past again, but he didn't appear. He got up the courage to head for the restaurant car to ask in there. As always happened when he crossed between carriages, he thought blackly about throwing himself under the train. In the restaurant car, he headed over to the steward. He hated asking strangers for information, exposing his ignorance about how things worked. He blamed himself. If he had known the schedule, he wouldn't have put himself in the position of having to ask questions. Rami faltered at first, then asked his question. With an indifferent air, the steward told him it would arrive seven minutes late. Rami thanked him warmly, but the steward still didn't look in his direction. Rami went back to his seat, looking at the passengers sitting either side as he passed, trying as best he could to seem agreeable. He gathered his jacket around him again to hide his scruffy clothes. He smiled at a child, who simply frowned back. He found his seat again and sat down to wait out the rest of the journey.

When Rami thought it through again, it was all only natural, logical—inevitable even. It was always going to have happened, as he saw that now. The only question had been when. If he had been smart he would have had prepared for it, rather than lose all control and find himself homeless with fourteen dollars to show from his thirty years of working and saving. What really hurt him was the girls, the way they had treated him. He knew why, but it was totally unjustified. They hadn't needed to do what they did, or say what they said. Especially Sasha. Marta had always been a little crazy, but Sasha was rational, so how could she have judged him in that way? How could she think he would ever want to harm her or her sister? That's what he couldn't understand, and what he would never accept.

He had asked himself nearly every day since how his daughters could blame him for having the feelings he had, for wanting to move on in his life, to find a happier place. He'd encouraged them all their lives to go after whatever made them happy. How could his own pursuit of that ever be a threat to them or to their mother? If he'd fought with Maria, well, that ought to have been something just between them. Why had the girls sided with their mother like that? He blamed them a great deal, but he blamed himself even more for not being able to explain his side of things in a way they could understand. He'd never been very good at expressing his feelings. Whenever he had to talk to them about that kind of stuff, he always became tongue-tied. Words failed him. He always wanted to say so many things, but all he ended up saying were a few terse, unhelpful words. And so the response he received would be equally abrupt and unaccommodating. And then the conversation would be over. Something in his way of doing things was a conversation killer. Maria had told him that at least a thousand times, and he knew she was right.

What Rami didn't find logical, inevitable, natural even, was losing his job at the same time. True, people say that it never rains but it pours, but then people say a lot of other things; they also say it's always darkest before the dawn. He wondered if that second one was going to come true. All those years working for one company. All the troubles it had been through and all he had done to make it a success. All the relationships he'd built up with the board members, with the executives, with his other colleagues. And then they fired him, just like that. It was like some bad B movie. Rami was a translator, though his real job title was grander: senior writer. Rami had never been able to come up with a good translation for the word *senior* in Arabic, which was an ironic reminder of the absurdity of his work. His job as senior writer had basically entailed translating advertisements and promotional material into Arabic, to make them fit the Arab market and the tastes of its consumers. He'd done that for what seemed an endless procession of clients, sometimes for the full range of their products, and other times for one-off lines. He'd written promotional copy for all kinds of products: diapers, cell phones, soda, real estate, watches, weight-loss clinics, massage parlors, chocolate bars, cars. Dozens and dozens of products and services. He'd sat at his desk each morning not knowing what would drop onto it that day. A new model of a car or a suppository, maybe. Heat-resistant overalls, perhaps. Whatever it was, his job was to be creative, to find something enticing about it. The file he'd be given would have the promotional material in English and he had to wrack his brains to work out how to tailor it to the Gulf market, the Egyptian market, the Libyan market, wherever.

And he was a master at it. Sometimes he even managed to expand the market for products or found ways to connect with new customers in the Middle East. That was what he did when the company had sent Mark and him to Jordan for a year. And yet the company had chosen to forget all that and terminate his contract. He went to work one day and was called in to see the boss, who told him the economic crisis meant they were going to have to let him go. He didn't want to go. He asked what translation had to do with the economic crisis, but his boss told him many clients were cutting back in Middle Eastern markets because of it. They couldn't justify keeping him on anymore. His boss smiled as he said it. Rami said the kind of things you're meant to say at these times, but what was happening was almost more insulting than he could bear. He kept up his smile to retain what was left of his pride, waved his arms around like a good sport, then swept the stuff off his desk into a box and left. The joke was that Maria managed, with her lawyer's help of course, to get her hands on his severance. That's why he'd been sitting on a train for sixteen hours, with fourteen dollars in his pocket and a big suitcase with only a few clothes inside, going to see a man he hadn't seen for years, in a city where he barely knew anyone.

His life had collapsed in exactly one year, but the last three months had been the toughest. The divorce was finalized six months after Maria had taken matters into her own hands. He lost everything in those six months. The court barred him from going within five hundred yards of Maria and his daughters for one year, an order that was subject to renewal. He'd lived off his last six hundred dollars for the last three months, including having to pay for his train ticket to New York. He'd stayed in the room of a friend who was working away from Miami for three months and who had offered to let him stay rent free until he could sort himself out. He cut back on all nonessentials, like the subway, phones, eating out, going to the movies, that kind of thing. He cut down on high-end food like meat, fruit, breakfast cereal. He'd managed to live on five dollars a day that way, but had no idea what he was going to do when those three months were up. Yesterday, the last day he could stay at his friend's place, Mark had phoned out of the blue.

He hadn't seen or talked to Mark for over two years, but they had become good friends when they worked together in the Middle East several years ago. Neither had needed anybody's help back then. Mark always introduced himself as a double minority, with a Catholic mother and a Jewish father. Yet his only connection with Judaism was his surname—Neumann—and his rudimentary knowledge of Hebrew, which had been enough to convince their company to send him to Israel to do some client marketing. That was the same time that Rami was going to Jordan for a year to market the same products in Arab countries.

Their workloads hadn't overlapped much, but they built up a good rapport, working out of a small rented office in Amman, and achieved a lot for the company. Mark hated staying in Israel, complaining how he didn't get on with his colleagues and how he often ended up in endless arguments with them, so he decided to stay in Amman, which was a peaceful place with nice people. Rami admired him for that, but what he really liked was Mark's unique ability to draw him out of his habitual reserve. Mark spoke with unabashed frankness about his problems with his family, religion, and the opposite sex, as well as his problems with life and work in the States, so much so that Rami ended up forgetting he was an American. Rami started to relax in his company and open up, and they ended up spending most of their time together in Amman and other places in Jordan that Rami hadn't known existed. They lived and worked together, and racked up small fortunes for themselves out of their business successes. It was a period that left both of them with many happy memories. Shortly after they went back to America, Mark had a falling out with his boss and left to work for a competitor. They lost track of one another after that. Rami got caught up in his work, his family, and all that went along with it.

And then Mark had phoned Rami's friend, the owner of the apartment in Miami, and got Rami instead. Mark asked him what he was doing sharing their friend's room, and Rami dropped his usual pride and confessed to all he had been through in the last year. Mark offered him a place to stay in Brooklyn right away, for as long as he liked. He could do some translation work for Mark's company. There was always a company press release or something like that that needed translating. Maybe he could translate some pieces for the company website too. Mark's company worked with Gulf corporations and some-times needed things translated quickly. They would be small jobs, but Rami would make a little money. He could maybe do five or six a month and make around a thousand dollars: not bad in times like these. Then, who knew? Maybe something else would turn up. Something always did if you knew the right people. And Mark knew a lot of people.

The apartment was big, so they wouldn't get in each other's way. Mark had bought a red pickup recently, and Rami could use it when Mark wasn't around. Mark told him not to worry about it. What were friends for if not times like these? He was so warm and genuine, just like he'd been in Amman, and Rami didn't exactly have other options, so he accepted.

He contacted his old professor before he set off for New York to see if he would be around, and accepted his invitation to go to Salma's birthday dinner. Rami was relieved, feeling as if he was his old self again, someone with friends to be with and places to go. With the train ticket using up most of his remaining money, he was on his way to New York, but now he was going to miss out on the party, and maybe Mark. Never had it poured so much for Rami.

It crossed his mind to ask Professor Darwish for a job, but he soon ditched that idea. He didn't dare, however difficult things were. He couldn't debase himself to that extent. His friendship with Mark made accepting a favor from him palatable, but Professor Darwish was another matter. He had to hold on to some standing among those who knew and respected him. He couldn't lose that. And anyway, Professor Darwish wouldn't give him a job after all that had happened in the past, even if he could. No, he couldn't ask for his help. But maybe he could ask Salma.

Salma had gotten to know Sasha when she spent the summer in New York. It was true they weren't close, but they hung out together when they were young. Sasha would always want to come with him when he visited Professor Darwish, and she knew Salma would be there too. The two girls liked spending time together, even though Salma could only speak the odd broken sentence of English back then, and of course Sasha didn't speak Arabic. They played happily enough together, though, and often without real toys. A doll would do. He had liked the fact that the two spent time together, because he thought it might just make a little Egyptian out of Sasha, or at least help her to make friends with other Egyptian girls. Maria encouraged the friendship too, mainly because she could get Sasha off her hands for a few days that way. Whenever Rami took the family on vacation to Egypt, the two girls would meet up without their mothers, who had arranged it all in advance over the phone. As Salma grew up, her mother stopped visiting New York, for some reason Rami didn't understand, but the two girls kept in touch, messaging each other now and again.

He didn't know where Salma stood on all of this, or if she even knew about it, but he wanted to ask her what she thought. Maybe she could help; perhaps convince Sasha that he had meant no harm to her or her sister. He'd never have abducted them back to Egypt. That would have been monstrous. Madness. If he could win Salma over, maybe she could convince Sasha he had meant well, and maybe remind her that he was her father after all. At the very least she could pass on his love to Sasha and her crazy sister, in spite of everything. If he could maybe convince Salma, then Sasha and Marta could be won over, and he could see them again after he'd settled in with Mark in Brooklyn, after he'd found work, after he could stand on his own two feet again. But what was he going to do now? Maybe he could see Salma in the morning, if she wasn't going straight back to Egypt. Surely she would be staying for at least a day after the party.

But would Mark still be waiting for him? What if he couldn't get hold of Mark? Where would he go?

All these questions. He just had to stop torturing himself; there was nothing he could do about it now. The last year had been a nightmare, but it had freed him of his inner anxieties. When the worst happens to you, there's not much left to be afraid of. Rami had come to realize over the course of the last year that he'd lived his whole life up to that point in fear. Fear he had concealed even from himself. After everything collapsed around him, he realized that fear had controlled everything he had done. He had worked and struggled, built up good relationships with everyone around him. He had dodged problems, stuck to the rules, steered clear of anything that would put him at odds with law or convention.

He had filed his tax returns honestly, paid every bill on time, and never got a speeding ticket. He never permitted loud music in his house, took out the trash on time, and only had parties on weekends. He never lit a campfire outside the permitted zones or barbecued on the beach. He never did anything you could remotely call breaking the rules. He had always figured that doing that would endear him to the system, give him protection. And so he wouldn't end up like immigrants sometimes do: out of a job, on the streets, their lives in pieces around them. But that was exactly what had happened. Maria, who was always sharper and quicker off the mark than him, had exploited the system and bent the rules her way, and he was left out in the cold, his life a car crash. No one had stepped up for him. No one had stood up for him. Even the guy at the neighborhood store wouldn't let him take his groceries on credit when the ATM turned his card down. They had all turned their backs on him, just like he'd always feared they would.

In the middle of all this, amid all this drama, he had paused more than once to look back on what had happened. Had it all really been inevitable? Couldn't he have turned back somehow? If Maria had only understood him to begin with, instead of threatening all kinds of revenge, maybe things wouldn't have turned out as they had. If Marta had not behaved so badly from the start of all this, egged on by Maria, things might have been different. If he hadn't found out that Maria had secretly taped their conversations, he wouldn't have insisted on the divorce the way he initially did. But one thing led to another, and now he found himself on this train to New York.

Over the last three months, after he stopped challenging the court rulings in his wife's favor, he surrendered to the new reality, and actually found some comfort in it. He decided then he'd do what everyone had accused him of wanting to do all along and go back to Egypt. He rationed food for a couple of days to buy an international phone card and called his brother in Cairo. The first call lasted forty-six minutes, during which time Rami explained what had happened over the last nine months. He told his brother he was determined to come back to Egypt. They talked over what he could do if he went back. They then agreed that Rami would phone back in a week, after his brother had looked into a few things to help Rami make a decision.

Rami spent that week planning his return. He spent most of the first day in the park, writing down the names of all the people he knew in Cairo in a little notebook, when he'd last met or spoken to them, and the last whereabouts he had for them. The following day, he went to the public library and searched online for job opportunities in Egypt, looking through the various PR and advertising firms' websites. He wrote down the kind of things he might do, and the names and addresses of places he'd need to check out. On the third day, he made notes on places he could live. Of course he'd live with his brother to begin with, or perhaps in the small old apartment they had in Alexandria, until he got himself sorted out. There was also the house where his parents had lived in the Kubri al-Qubba district in Cairo. Maybe it would be better to live there. He made a note to ask his brother about that. He had sixteen minutes left on the phone card. He thought about buying another, but decided against it at the last minute. He'd keep the call to the sixteen minutes he had left and buy another card the next time. That meant he could spend the ten dollars he would have wasted on a second card to feed himself for a couple of days. In the end, the call only lasted six minutes, leaving Rami ten minutes on the card he still carried in his wallet.

Rami was a polite, amenable guy who hated confrontation and tended to find excuses for others, but that didn't mean he was an idiot. He worked out in the first minute of the call what his brother was trying to say. After ninety seconds of his brother's dithering, Rami asked straight out if he was trying to say he shouldn't come back. His brother seemed relieved he no longer had to beat around the bush. Rami gave him one more minute to explain himself. His brother took two to explain why Rami's return in these circumstances would be a disaster: if he returned as a failure, it would put the family in a difficult position socially. And Rami wouldn't be able to stand on his own two feet in a market he understood nothing about and without the necessary professional experience in Egypt. At his age, he'd find it impossible to fit back in, having lived most of his life as an American. When Rami asked about their parents' house, his brother replied edgily that that was a minor consideration and wouldn't solve the real problem. He was welcome to stay with them as long as he wished, as a guest, but settling back down in Egypt was another matter. What he wanted to do wouldn't work out well for him. Rami thanked him for his honesty, agreed to keep in touch, and ended the call before he hit the seventh minute.

Rami thought all of this over, shaking his head in disbelief at how his life had turned out. He hitched his jacket around him for the umpteenth time and looked apprehensively out of the train window. The young girl had gotten out in New Jersey. The car seemed almost empty as it entered New York's Penn Station. He wondered again what he would do if he didn't find Mark waiting outside Professor Darwish's house. The agreement was that Mark would pick Rami up after dinner, just before midnight. It was midnight now: what if Mark left before he got there? What if Mark had checked with Professor Darwish, who had told him Rami hadn't showed up? Mark would think he'd changed his plans, and go home by himself. Where would Rami spend the night? Where could Rami go with his last fourteen dollars? He had no other money, no credit card, nothing at all. He didn't even know where Mark lived.

Rami's mind was working overtime as the train halted on the platform. He couldn't ask Professor Darwish. He didn't dare, knowing the professor didn't like doing that kind of thing at all. Maybe he could find a cheap hotel, and then find work to pay for it afterward. But who would give him a job? He'd tried in Miami and only got sneers in return. He couldn't even get a bar job. No experience. And no one wanted a middle-aged, Arab-looking, Arab-sounding guy. Maybe he could get a job flipping burgers. No one would pick up on his accent in the kitchen. No customers or their kids frowning when they couldn't understand what he said. But it would take time to find a job. He thought over whether there was anyone else there who could help him. Or should he swallow what was left of his pride, knock on Professor Darwish's door in the middle of the night, and ask him to put him up for the night? Then, in the morning, he could ask Darwish to help him find work. But even if he plucked up the courage to do that, nobody would answer the door at that time of night. Perhaps he could he sleep in Central Park. Fourteen dollars might last him three days if he slept in the park, but then what? He went around and around in circles; his thoughts were chasing their own tails.

The few remaining passengers were quickly getting off the train as Rami dragged himself and his half-empty suitcase along. The other passengers were either met by someone or headed off purposefully in one particular direction. Rami hesitated. He walked haltingly, as if didn't want to walk at all, putting off going out into the station concourse and facing his unknown fate. He feared what the next few hours would bring, and what choices he would end up having to make. He dragged his case with heavy steps, and was scarcely able to look beyond the platform to the concourse, but kept going. He had to. He cast a glance at the darkened station concourse ahead. Maybe he'd see Mark waiting there. But what made him think Mark would come to the station? He fretted again about whether he had given Darwish's correct address to

Mark. He looked quickly around the concourse, but there was no one there but him. Of course there wasn't. The restaurants were closed and the lights dimmed. He thought about picking up his pace to catch the subway to Professor Darwish's place, but couldn't work out where the line was. Every passageway he took was closed. Maybe he could spend the night there on a bench, and see Professor Darwish and Salma in the morning. Then he could try to track down Mark.

He thought it over and decided to look around Penn Station for somewhere to wait until morning.

4

Goliath's Eye

I LEFT MY CAR AND took the train. There are no parking spots around here, and the museum closes at five—the worst of the rush hour. When I'm done here, I'll take the train back and stay at the mosque until the sunset-prayer lesson. Then I'll pick up Amira and go to dinner at her sister's ex-husband's. May God forgive her for roping me into that dinner. He and I don't get along. I won't be a very pleasant guest, grumbling about being there, about the people I'm sitting with, and about the way they act. They'll be uncomfortable having us there. We might swap inane observations on how busy it is everywhere or what weather we're having, or start conversations that end up more like quarrels. To me there's nothing worse than being around Americanized Arabs. I'd rather talk to actual Americans. And he's the sheikh of Americanized Arabs, that one. Years ago, I remember looking through a book of his that described the Arabs as having fallen out of history without having been buried. When I first met him I asked him about it, and the ensuing discussion might have ended in someone being strangled if Amira hadn't stepped in.

Why is she dragging me to dinner at that man's house? She says it's Salma's birthday party, and Leila wants us there. Since her sister died, Amira treats Leila like she's her own daughter. My God, I can't make any sense of that family. That idiot Professor Darwish, who hates Muslims and hates himself. His daughter, Leila, is the complete opposite, but

69

no less forceful. The granddaughter, Salma, is lost, and her father and her uncle do nothing about it. Her mother allowed her to travel to America alone, on the basis that her father was here, yet she insisted the girl stay with her grandfather, who she hates and because of whom she left America altogether. Then she involves us in this squabble, insisting her aunt keep watch over her daughter, as if we're private eyes or something. Amira refuses Leila nothing, however extravagant the demand. God have mercy on them. Women were good-hearted, but weak-minded.

I'll call in at the mosque before this damned dinner party. A young man came to me when afternoon prayers were over, asking to speak about a personal matter. He's sure to be looking for a wife. I'll ask Amira if she can think of anyone.

I left Fulton Street Station and walked toward the little museum set up by the fire department. They say they'll build a bigger one later. We'll see. When I got to the museum, I found a fire truck parked near the visitors' entrance. A few men stood in front of it, gazing in wonder, as if it had fallen from the sky or was about to ascend into it. I paid the seven dollars and went through the automatic barrier. I wondered what they do with this money. I wandered around the galleries for a little while, looking at the walls, the pendants, the collections, the banners, the names, the photographs. I glanced at them briefly, then sat on one of the benches that ran down the middle of the gallery.

What kind of miserable museum was this? If they had left it to me, I'd have done ten times better. A real museum, with real exhibits: the pens and paper used to write out the original idea, the clothes worn by those who had planned the attack, the rugs they sat on, the teacups they sipped from as they pondered the obstacles, the phones they used, the passports, the emails, the cameras, the bank accounts, the disguises, the training equipment, the boarding passes, the baggage checks with the names of the perpetrators on them. Everything they'd used to do this.

I know what really happened. I know the whole story. I know where the necessary information came from to organize an attack of this complexity. How they got hold of the money and from where. How they were recruited and trained; how all the pieces of the puzzle were put together to make it happen so perfectly. I read the US authorities' report on the incident, and laughed inside. I heard all the Arab accusations about America, and laughed to myself too. Each side tries to exonerate itself, and pin the blame on the other.

But I know the truth: what happened, the parts played by those who were mentioned in the investigation, and the parts played by those who were not.

I sit in this memorial, looking at the pictures and exhibits, the words written and pictures displayed of some of those who died, the tributes of their family and loved ones. It has no effect on me at all. I am a monster. I rejoiced in the attack. I felt an overwhelming sense of revenge wash over me, diminished only by the resilience of the Twin Towers that allowed so many to survive. I wanted all seventy-five thousand of them dead. Don't talk to me about the dead; I don't want to hear anything about them. I look at the faces on the walls, and the comments from their families: "We miss you, Jimmy." "Thinking of you, Lizzie." "Rebecca, you'll be in my heart forever." Hollow words. Meaningless. No one lasts forever. We all die. Another dead woman or two—what's the difference? These victims: I know nothing about them. People perish like everything else does. God will have mercy on them, if it's mercy they deserve, and He'll punish them if they deserve it. Death means nothing. How many people die every day? How many are dying at this very moment, this very second? Do we build a museum for them? Did these people have any more right to survive than others? Do they have the right to live longer than those who died before them? This was their appointed time. This was their life. This was their appointment with death. No one brings that forward or moves it back. Whether they died here, or under the wheels of a car, or from food that gave them cancer, or from a bomb exploding or an earthquake, it is all predestined. I know nothing about any of these people, and I don't want to know. If I had to kill them with my own hands, I wouldn't have hesitated. But it was written that some would survive, as it was written that some would die. And I am not in the business of feeling sorry for them.

What is all this trash they've put in here? All that destruction from the Twin Towers and they can only find this junk. Why don't they add the cluster bombs that killed my father? Or the flares that lit up the face of my mother so that her killer could murder her?

I'd heard about this museum, so I came to see it for myself. I wondered who the other visitors were. I didn't think they'd be the victims' families. If my son had been killed like that, I wouldn't come here to be reminded of it. Do the bereaved really need a memorial like this, or is it for those fantasists who need a tragedy to feel empathy for? Or maybe there were people who came to rejoice secretly at the slap in the face of imperialism. Maybe schoolchildren are brought here to plant hatred in them.

I can hear the sound of the documentary the museum founders have running. They have changed it into a kind of place of worship, made it into another Pearl Harbor. The narrator says that the Twin Towers symbolized world peace, because trade creates peace. And what peace!

Visitors pass by, looking at me with suspicion. They must be wondering what that Arab is doing here. Schadenfreude? Exulting in the acts of his kind? A little boy's gaze lingers on me as he clings more tightly to his dad. I'm no different from the rest, those you'll come across when you go outside, on trains aboveground and below, in workplaces, in your houses, among your women. We're all the same in your eyes: me in my gray suit and trimmed, gray-flecked beard, short in stature and faint of voice; another with a straggly beard, short jilbab, an angry, foreign appearance, and a bellowing voice; a third in shorts and with a glass of beer in his hand. You're scared of us all. Make us all one man; unite us. Your hatred feeds our resolve.

I could sit here and play the victim. I could lecture you about America's crimes. I could tell you tales of Beirut—refugee camps and what lies under the rubble of houses bombed by high-tech death planes that fly the banner of "trade brings peace." I am the survivor of massacres that crushed all those I loved. I could tell you about massacres, assassinations, killings out of spite, and killings out of error. I could tell you poignant tales of civilians targeted in order to terrorize, to coerce, to cheer one spirit or break another. I could tell you about your plane that dipped and arced in the skies, while some raw recruit hopelessly fired his 16mm at it, only for it to return and bombard the whole neighborhood in West Beirut. Did that pilot think about the inhabitants: the civilians, the innocents? Did he really think that the dumb owner of the 16mm was a real threat? Or did he believe, deep in his heart, that these people were worthless; that he could kill them all and it would mean nothing? Did he do it because of some evil within him or was he just following orders?

It was me who fired the 16mm, knowing damn well that it couldn't damage the plane. I was absolutely sure the plane would come back and bomb the whole neighborhood. I wanted to wake up those who were still deluded that the West was humane and had principles. People would see the naked truth with their own eyes. They would realize the extent to which they were on their own against those monsters. Then they'd understand that they had no choice but to fight, to defend themselves, or die at the hands of the Western invader who understands only force.

I have never had any illusions on that score. Yet I had patience with those who called for truces and dialogue, those who claimed there were Westerners who would accept us, and espoused the end of enmity between us. Their claims were all lies. I was patient with them. I tolerated their self-delusion and their self-humiliation at the feet of the West; waiting for it to open the door to them. All they got was humiliation, time after time, and yet they didn't understand.

I could tell you tales of women and children looking for water to drink in the basements, without knowing what would kill them first—thirst, or rage at the Americans and Europeans who had promised to protect them but had then abandoned them, or despair, or an American shell that would relieve them of their misery.

I can tell you tales of civilians who stayed in Sabra and were killed by those brutes in their own homes, one by one, while the Israel "Defense" Forces surrounded the area and fired American-made flares to illuminate the dark sky for the killers. Shame on the guard and the guarded.

I can tell you tales of the killers that ran out of bullets in the house I was hiding in, and so carried on with knives. I survived only because they threw my mother's body on top of me after they'd slaughtered her. I hid under her body, feeling it stiffen and grow cold, little by little.

But I don't want to tell you any of these tales. I don't want your false pity; pity that is good for nothing. I never trusted you or your promises. And when I refused to leave with those who did, I knew you and your proxies would come after us. I knew you would make us pay, because we stood in the way of you and your proxies, because we said no. I who was fighting you survived; your soldiers killed my defenseless, unarmed mother. So don't talk to me about the sanctity of civilians' lives. I have never deluded myself about that. I expect nothing less from you. I was born a fighter in a camp where your bombs rained down from the sky for whole seasons. I picked off those of you that I could. That's how I've lived my life. I know your soldiers, they know me, and we all know the rules of the game. So let no one talk to me about respect for the lives of the innocent. Your soldiers don't give a damn about that, and nor do I. Innocent civilians are the victims, the casualties of war, and they die when they have to. They die on top of me today, and on top of you tomorrow. You who are looking at me now from behind these memorabilia, ask yourself how we will next meet. Will it be you standing over my corpse, or you flat on your back, trying to make out my face as you die in agony?

Two days ago Salma confessed to Amira, almost proudly, that she had stolen a book from the neighborhood library. Amira was shocked, and demanded she take it back immediately. Salma was surprised: hadn't we always told her we were at constant war with the crusader West? Amira spent two hours with her, explaining. This is Brooklyn, not a battlefield. Salma didn't understand and asked me about it, without mentioning the stolen book. Such misunderstanding is common. I told her I couldn't take out a weapon and wound my neighbor in this country, whatever his persuasion was, because he has rights as my neighbor, but I would kill him in battle without hesitation. I don't know if she understood.

Those of you who stare at me amid these ridiculous exhibits, my fellow passengers on the subway or in the street: you have rights as a neighbor, just like the man who lives opposite me in Brooklyn: the one I send cookies to at Eid and who sends me a present at Christmas. But when the call to arms comes, you're no longer neighbors. This makes you mad, doesn't it, but why should it? What would you do, in Iraq or Afghanistan, if you found me, your neighbor, sitting smoking shisha where one of your missiles was going to strike? Would you stop everything and warn me to get out of harm's way?

It's close to five and I can't hang around any longer. Visitors have come and gone more than once, but I'm still sitting here. Yet it's difficult for me to leave this place; it's as if these exhibits were my property, as if this were part of my home. Still, I must go. I have to go back to the mosque in Brooklyn, and then to this dinner party. I wouldn't go if it weren't for Amira's insistence and my love for Salma. She's good-hearted, that girl. Despite her faults, she has a raw goodness to her. She's hard-working, dogged, and eager to learn. It's been a long time since I met a girl with such a longing for education. Sharp-witted, pure-hearted, seemingly undamaged by her parent's divorce. Maybe she inherited her seriousness and thirst for knowledge from Grandpa Darwish, the professor. He may have abused his talent, but maybe his granddaughter will go down the right road. Amira is trying to convince her to stay here, and maybe I could swing a scholarship for her and talk her into it. Amira says her mother, Leila, might support it too. Her mother is the key. Her grandfather is gaga, and nobody cares what he thinks anymore. Her father has no say in it. May God reward you well, Amira, if you pull it off. A girl with those abilities can turn into a force for good, if she's re-educated, guided back into the fold. Amira could do that, God willing. I'll see her father and grand-father this evening. I won't say anything about this to them, though. Amira warned me not to. We don't want to seem any keener on the idea than necessary. It's Amira's job to convince the girl. Then we'll speak to her mother. Then, God willing, it'll all go ahead from there.

I used to think that we would fight on until we won. During the 1967 war, I buried what was left of my father's body, after he was blown apart by a cluster bomb. I left my mother and sister in the camp, and went to fight with those who had gone out to wage God's war. A twenty-year-old fighter. I fought in Jordan, Lebanon, places around Europe. For twenty years we ambushed you and for twenty years you ambushed us. We killed you and you killed us, in cold blood or not. If it was in an Arab country, it was mainly aerial bombardment that did the killing. If it was in Europe, it was in cold blood: a bullet to the skull from a pistol, a bomb blast, maybe. Whenever we fought you, you defeated us, only leaving us thirstier for revenge. We'd choose another battleground to inflict an even greater blow, but you did not retreat. You still found another way to come back and inflict a harsher punishment on us. You think our defeats will deter us from combat, but they never will. I used to complain to my commanders about our repeated defeats, but they would say that, though these blows hurt us, we would only be defeated when we left the battlefield. Our steadfastness was key to our hopes, and the beginning of our victory to come, however far away that might be. So where is that far-off victory? I have asked myself this dozens of times, in the camps, in the trenches, behind sandbags, in the trucks. I have concluded that victory will never come until we take the fight to your lands.

So I decided to come here, among you, into your very homes. You have fought on our lands for over a hundred years, and the time has come to bring the battle to yours. We are David and you are a tyrannical Goliath. David did not defeat Goliath by fighting him face to face. Goliath was bigger, stronger, better equipped for the duel, but David won by guile, by throwing a stone into the eye of the tyrant giant. We aim for your eye. We will deal you a fatal blow. I stood watching the Twin Towers collapse, and what gradually percolated through me was a feeling of ultimate victory. We had put all the pieces together; we had linked the rings in perfect concentricity. No one can truly comprehend the genius required to put together something like this, to put all these opposing forces into one scheme so that each one serves the other, without knowing each other or knowing what they're doing, but all working toward the same end result. This was genius incarnate, something never seen before. Who would believe we had gotten the wolf and the lamb to work together, complementing one another's work, neither one seeing or knowing of the other. We put the pieces together to form an almost mystical harmony. If it could be drawn, it would be more famous than Leonardo da Vinci's works. If it were music, it would be greater than

Beethoven's *Ninth*. It truly was the mother of all operations.

I stood watching the Twin Towers collapse, and how your leaders and your media shrieked. And as their shrieking rose, so too did their threats. It confirmed for me the depth of the pain you were suffering, and confirmed too your leaders' lack of guile.

I thought that all that screaming and yelling would give way to a recognition of what had just been inflicted on you. But they did not wake up to it. They went ahead with even more transgressions. This blow did not make them see the truth. In fact, it almost made their blindness greater. What kind of stupidity turns men away from the reason for their pain, makes them ascribe this pain to what should be the cure, and hence aggravates the pain further? I never imagined that this would be the way they would react. I said to myself this is just a passing moment, and then the reasonable voices will prevail and turn their attention to the root of the problem. But years have passed and nothing of the sort happened. Years have passed and nothing has happened at all. Nothing has changed. The blow was struck to Goliath's eye, but the pain did not turn him away from tyranny. He did not surrender as we had expected. In fact, his blindness made him more despotic.

I understood. At last I understood. You will never win, and we will never win. In fact, we will continue battling one another forever. We sink the knife into you, and you into us, but neither will fall to the ground dead. Neither of us will emerge the victor unless the other surrenders, and the other will never surrender. No suffering will deflect you from your tyranny, and no defeat will deflect us from our rights. The battle continues. There is a ceaseless, unending rhythm to our historic confrontation. All that remains is for us to keep wounding one another, unceasingly, unendingly. And so I stand here like a fork in your eye, and every fork in your eye is one less in ours. We are here to stay. Until our last days. And yours.

I have said good-bye to combat, but I'm still here to hurt you, and minimize the damage you cause to us. Nowadays, I preach respect for the law and nonviolence. I don't bear arms or advocate their use. I lead the prayers in our little Brooklyn mosque. I give lessons on Islamic law and the ways of the prophet to whoever wishes to listen. I arrange scholarships and jobs for young men, and righteous marriages. Nothing more than that. I don't train anyone to carry or use weapons, and I don't advise anyone to either. What I do is build character among our young men and women, bring them back to their roots, steer them from the clutches of the materialist world to which you hook them. I stop you controlling the young minds that blossom in your midst. I save them from forgetting who they are and where they come from and the fate you have in mind for them. I enlighten them about your hypocritical claims, and show them your double standards: one rule for us, another for you. I guide these young people and make sure they don't fall for your cheap propaganda about freedom and equality. I protect and shield them, and then leave them to choose their own paths. If they follow the path of jihad, if they find it within themselves to do that, someone will come and guide them through it. It won't be me, but others—others you don't see. They rise up out of your grasp and from behind your backs. So what are you doing about me and about them? Will you change your laws to tighten the noose around our necks? It will only prove what we have always said: that your talk of freedom and equality is all hypocrisy. You will crush those freedoms when you need to. Will you send us to your prisons, and become more distrustful of Arabs and Muslims? Will you stop our sons obtaining positions of influence?

Every knife you bury in us will only prove what we say about you, will only strengthen the determination of our young men and push them into dragging their rights out of you. Our strength derives from our weakness; we are the sons of David. You are the sons of Goliath; your weakness comes from your strength. Your hatred for us only binds us closer together, only makes us more steadfast. That in turn will make you warier of us, make you oppress us even more. We are a pair engaged in a deathly embrace that makes us both suffer. Let's see which of us can bear the pain better.

Five o'clock. I'll leave you now. I'll go to our mosque, then to Salma's dinner party. It's hard for me to leave this museum. I am the exhibit missing from the memorial of our endless battles here. If whoever runs this place wants to complete the list of exhibits, I can send you one of us to sit here on this wooden bench every day, to complete the picture, in the museum memorializing our shared fate.

5

Marieke

I STARED AT THE COMPUTER in disbelief. New York? Marieke, here in New York? After everything, we are both here— by chance! The memory of her came to me suddenly, like it does every year. She occupies my mind, so I write to her. It normally takes her a week to get back to me. This time it was within minutes. Her message and mine, with the same date, sitting next to one another in my inbox. I was still at my computer when her beautiful name appeared on the screen. M-a-r-i-e-k-e: those letters that fill my heart with joy, that leave every inch of me awash with tender thoughts. Marieke was in New York, and for a whole week. I fired back a short question: "Shall we meet?" I sent it before thinking through the consequences. I sat staring at the screen. A few minutes later, her name appeared again, and I opened the email with trepidation. "Yes," she said. "Where?" That brought a huge smile to my face. Forget the consequences: I was going to see her. I would see Marieke. As we exchanged emails, I became more and more exhilarated. We finally agreed to meet in the lobby of the hotel she was staying in on First and Forty-Ninth. At eight thirty, later that day.

What had I been thinking, suggesting a meeting? How could I see her again? How could I look at her? And how would we greet each other? Would we shake hands like strangers or kiss each other on the cheek like friends? And what would we talk about? Maybe about why I was in New York. I could tell her about my one-year hospital placement that was nearly over. She'd tell me what she'd been doing. She'd ask me about Egypt and about Salma, and I'd ask her how her life had been since her last email, a year ago. Did she go to Amsterdam as she'd planned, or stay in Leiden as she wanted? How was her little house? And then we'd fall silent and sip our drinks. Maybe the waiter would come over and ask us something, and then it'd be silence again. Would she ask me about my love life? Would I ask her about that Greek guy she mentioned in her emails? No, I didn't want to hear about him, or anybody else. Would we touch on the difficult stuff? Would we talk about us, about what had happened? We hadn't met face to face since that time when we were madly in love—since we agreed she would come over at Christmas and stay with me until we sorted ourselves out. We'd spoken on the phone once, and exchanged an email or two every year, but we'd never met up. I wondered if she would be different.

Ay Marieke, Marieke!

I got off at Fifty-First Street and headed for First Avenue. It was warm. I crossed the road and headed for the address she gave me. I rarely came to this part of town. I found the hotel immediately after the UN building. The UN was dark save for a few lights dotting the upper floors. What were they up to in the UN at this late hour? I entered the hotel. There was a small reception desk with one staff member behind it. I asked her where the lobby was, and she said I was in it. When I seemed to hesitate, she suggested I might find who I was looking for in the bar. I went through a little door to find a narrow rectangular restaurant overlooking the street. In the middle, toward the right, sat the wonderful Marieke on a semicircular couch with a man in his late fifties. Papers were scattered on the table in front of them, next to two drinks. Her dark-blond, shoulder-length hair, her thin, round glasses on her forehead, her wide smile, her lower lip twisted into a slight smirk, her rosy cheeks, and her pale, slightly reddish neck. She wore a white, man's shirt with a dark jacket over it, and I could see her black pants and shoes under the table. Her slim shoulders and shapely body that I recalled as if it were yesterday. It was the Marieke that I loved, despite all the years that had passed, and despite what she had done to me.

What was I thinking when I asked her to meet me?

She looked up from her papers toward the bar door, and saw me standing frozen to the spot. A smile came over her face, lighting it up even more. The man she was sitting with turned toward me, and put what seemed to be an attempt to flirt on hold. She got up and I walked toward her. A little disconcerted, she walked around the table toward me. Do I offer my hand or fling open my arms to her? She didn't hold back, though; she held out her arms and came in for a hug. A little unsettled, I hugged her back. We held each other for a little longer than friends normally do, then leaned our heads back slightly to see each other's faces without uncoupling our bodies. We gave each other all-knowing smiles. Loving smiles, acknowledging love, how complicated the world was, and how complicated we were ourselves—knowing, yielding smiles, resigned to our situation and rejecting it at the same time. We hugged again for a moment, then stepped apart slowly. She took me by the hand and introduced me to the man she was with: some guy, Dutch name, didn't catch it. Her boss. She introduced me by my first name: "Luqman. An old friend." He greeted me with unconvincing interest and uttered something about the endless work, how hardworking Marieke was, then gestured to her to go off with her friend, patting her on the shoulder. That choked me. How come he'd put his hand on her shoulder?

We sat at the end of the bar. I asked about her boss, and said he seemed a bit flirty. She laughed and said he was a ladies' man, but harmless because he was so obvious about it. Then she asked drily if I was jealous. I raised my hands in surrender and she laughed again, grabbed my hand, and pulled it back on top of the bar. She asked what I'd been up to in New York, so I told her. I asked her the same, and she told me about negotiations between two pharmaceutical companies, one of which she worked for, the regulatory authorities and the World Health Organization. I recalled reading something about these negotiations in the paper the day before and smiled, saying it had never entered my head when I read about it that it would lead me back to her. She smiled. I asked what was going on with her and she said she hadn't left Leiden, and still went to work in Amsterdam by train every day. She couldn't bear to leave that little town. I said I'd be really angry if she ever did, after all that had happened. Her eyes told me she knew what I meant, but didn't want to dwell on that topic, and she moved on to asking how I had been. I told her what had happened to me since we'd last emailed. I'd been living in New York. I loved the city and my apartment in Brooklyn. I told her about my daughter Salma's visit and how excited she was about the city; how she wanted to come and study here, and maybe even live with me if I decided to stay in New York. Marieke said it was a tough decision for a girl her age and asked me what I thought. I raised my hands, saying that the girl was asking herself the same questions I had been asking myself since I was her age. Marieke smiled in agreement.

She asked me about developments in Egypt, and we talked politics a little; then the topic moved on to Holland. She told me she'd joined the Christian Democratic Appeal Party, and was working on projects to integrate immigrants into the community in Leiden. I asked her how she was finding it, and she did not hide her frustration, saying she'd found out just how naïve she'd been when she thought political work was to serve the public interest. I stayed silent, thinking: didn't I tell you all of this, years ago?

We moved from one subject to another, talking about everything: what my job and my cancer research involved; her research on Egyptian and European politics; Arab and

Muslim migrants and the problems they faced with both state and society in Holland; US politics and the "war on terror"; my relationship with Salma, her complicated relationship with her mother, and her mother's complicated relationship with Salma's grandfather; Marieke's longing for kids, and her parents' and brothers' longing for her to have them; the house in Leiden; music; Bach. And Edward Said, whom we both loved, though had never met. I had had the chance to have dinner with him two months before, but had ended up missing it. She called me an idiot and laughed. She said it was undoubtedly one of my regular moments of stupidity. I didn't take the bait, and we carried on talking about everything—everything except us, that is. We didn't eat; we just spent three hours talking. The waiter came over to say they were closing soon, and suggested we go up to the restaurant on the top floor if we wanted to stay for the rest of the evening. She looked exhausted, so I suggested we end the evening there. She nodded and said she hadn't slept well since she'd flown in. We fell silent, neither of us knowing exactly where we stood. She asked me if I was on shift tomorrow. I said I wasn't. She said her negotiating meeting wasn't due to start until eleven in the morning, and suggested we have breakfast together. I agreed straightaway and suggested a new restaurant near my house in Brooklyn. We agreed to meet in front of Brooklyn Bridge Station at eight. I kissed her on the cheek and left.

My cell phone rang as I came off Cairo's October 6th Bridge. I recognized the number, pulled over, and answered it. Her sweet voice seemed a little more hesitant than normal. It was November and traces of early morning rain were spattered on the road. Passing cars left dirty spray behind them on my windscreen. She said she couldn't come for Christmas. She said things I didn't understand, about needing to know herself better before she could commit to anyone. I asked her to help me understand and she said she would explain everything in a letter, but had wanted to hear my voice and tell me in person. I asked her to come and tell me in person, face to face. She laughed and said that my voice over the phone was good enough for now. She said she'd thought it over a lot, and that it was the toughest decision she had ever had to make. She said she knew for sure that she loved me, and that we were soul mates. She was ready right then to be with me forever, but knew that was impossible, because she was who she was and I was who I was. If we tried to escape ourselves so as to be together, we would lose ourselves. "You can't live in Leiden, and I can't live in Cairo. We both have plans we can only make work in our own countries . . . and my turning up would complicate your relationship with Salma . . . and the religious thing, the difference . . . I want to bring up my kids as Christians."

I kept objecting, and she kept insisting. I appealed to her heart, her mind, her emotions. I said everything I could think of, parked on the side of Salah Salim Street, the passing cars drenching me in dirty rainwater, but she was unmovable. "It's the age-old dilemma," she said. "Love and the impossible." She started crying, then hung up. And there I was, sitting alone on Salah Salim, more alone than I had ever been before.

We met at eight on the dot at Brooklyn Bridge Station. Neither of us had slept well, yet both of us were wide awake. We were in a state of joy that can only be explained by what united us, and what we avoided mentioning. We wanted to make the most of our being together. We had breakfast. We made a celebration out of it. We exulted in our food. "This yogurt . . . oh my God! . . . This coffee, can you believe it? . . . This seeded brown bread with the eggs, the salmon . . . It's too much! . . . There's fruit salad, cheese—all kinds of cheeses, orange juice, strawberries, blackberries, real ones, you know? . . . This restaurant is amazing!" We breakfasted as if it were every breakfast we could have ever had together. We felt increasingly at ease with one another, which led us toward dangerous territory in our conversation. She praised the restaurant, then added playfully that it was almost as good as our breakfasts in Leiden. I smiled and said, "Almost. But we need more practice to get back to that level." She laughed and asked if I remembered the pasta we had cooked at her place. I replied that it'd had black olives and broccoli in it, and when she seemed surprised I remembered such detail I gave her a reproachful look, but didn't pursue it.

She eventually plucked up the courage to ask about my love life. I shrugged, indicating there was no one worth mentioning. I was quiet for a little while, then asked her about the Greek guy. She smiled and shook her head. "It never went beyond the affair I mentioned in my email. . . . He wasn't serious. We had no spiritual connection that we could build on."

She shot me a glance, wanting to know if I understood. I nodded and we said no more about it. I wanted to ask her about our spiritual connection and what good it did us, but I hesitated. I didn't want to spoil the pleasure of the moment. But it managed to spoil itself.

The old pain returned: the same pain that shot through me when she said she wouldn't come to Cairo; the same pain that shot through me every time we spoke about our love and came to the same conclusion about its impossibility. How many times had I thought about cutting her off just to avoid this? And now, by my own free will, I meet up with her. Did I think we would finally agree and live happily ever after? What am I doing to myself? How can I go back to my hopeless life now, having reopened the old wounds with my own two hands? She was smarter than me, thought further ahead: did she hope, like me, that we would work it out, that we'd end up back together?

It was nearly ten thirty. We both knew it was time to go.

"What time do you finish work today?" I asked.

"Not before ten, but I could get away by five tomorrow."

"Do you have any plans?"

"No. What about Salma? Aren't you meeting up with her tomorrow?"

"No, she's in DC."

"Let's meet up, then."

"Definitely."

She took my arm as we left the restaurant. We exchanged kisses like friends, and she headed off. I stood watching her until she entered the subway, then went to the hospital.

We'd met for the first time in the same city, exactly seven years before, in a workshop organized by the university. I was taken with her as soon as I laid eyes on her, but I was dating someone else, so I didn't pursue it. She told me later that she had been taken with me the first time we'd met too, and had tried to find out where I stood. I'd let her know, unintentionally, that I was with someone. I didn't remember doing that, but she insisted I used to get a lot of phone calls, and once, when the phone rang while I was talking with her, I'd smiled apologetically and told her it was "my better half," so she kept quiet. Nothing happened between us other than this hidden mutual attraction, one laden with possibilities but set aside. A few months later, she sent me some pictures taken at the workshop. A year later, I messaged her, and everyone else in the group, about some research I was doing on a topic we'd discussed in our workshop, and she replied, congratulating me. A whole year after that, she messaged me to say that she'd suggested one of her colleagues, who was spending several weeks posted to a Cairo hospital, contact me. Things developed from there.

It was late August when her email arrived telling me her friend was coming to Cairo. The scorching weather was enough to drive one to despair. In the midst of a heat wave, sweating away in my little apartment, I replied jokingly, asking what kind of relationship she had with this friend of hers. She took me seriously, replying that she was straight, and that it infuriated her so many people thought she was into women. She asked why I did. I hadn't thought she'd take something I'd said in jest seriously, so I said that maybe it was the aloof way she dealt with men that might have made me suspect as much. She shot a reply straight back, saying she'd give up hope if that's what I thought, since she had been attracted to me and thought she had let me know as much. She added that she couldn't believe it hadn't entered my head, to the point that I'd thought she must prefer women. Then she asked me if I was still dating that other woman. Just like that. She added a half-apology for being so direct, something she called being "typically Dutch."

This "typically Dutch" email was followed by 730 others over the course of a year, as we averaged roughly an email each per day. These emails were shared confessions—almost feverish, and about all kinds of things. We discussed every subject imaginable with complete honesty, to the point that it was painful at times. Nothing was off-limits. We each divulged our deepest fears about ourselves and others, writing about everything we considered a failing in ourselves, the dreams we had abandoned, and those we didn't normally dare give voice to. We disclosed the sins we had committed, and those we wished we had. It was as if we had stripped away every mask, dropped every pretense. Our words were transparent, even brutal, and our honesty amazed us both. We mastered the art of candor, through three-hundred-some confessions on either side. We opened our hearts in a way neither of us had before, maybe because we thought we'd never meet again. Yet, at the same time, we became addicted to one another. I can barely remember anything from that year other than nights in front of the computer, reading and writing.

Then I suggested we meet, without thinking it through, just like I had today. She asked me what for, and I replied: so that we didn't spend the rest of lives wondering what would have happened if we did. She agreed, on the condition we were just meeting up, nothing more. She suggested meeting in Venice, but I asked why she wouldn't come to Cairo.

She said taking a trip to another country to meet a man was a massive step, one she couldn't take within the limits we had set ourselves. Besides, neither of us had visited Venice before, so it could be just "a trip to Venice" for both of us. I laughed and said this was a complicated business, and that I had no problem flying to visit a woman and was happy to go meet her in Holland. She liked this, and didn't object. We agreed I'd visit her in her little town of Leiden in the third week of September. She announced in her typically Dutch way that I would be sleeping in my own room and nothing would happen between us. I joked that we couldn't really get to know each other if we didn't breach this barrier that bars men and women from understanding one another. I said if we really wanted to understand each other's feelings, whether they went beyond just physical attraction, we ought to have sex and settle the matter altogether. We would see afterward if we really needed to be together. She informed me that was a cheap old trick. "No sex. You'll sleep in your own room." That was just how it was.

I took the train from Schiphol Airport to Leiden. When I got off, I found this amazing blond-haired woman waiting for me with a broad smile and open arms. She was wearing something white, with a short blue denim jacket over the top and black pants. Her hair was shorter than when I'd first met her in New York, cut above the shoulder. We gazed at each other for a long time. Our smiling expressions said so many things, like: have we both lost our minds? Are you really here? Could this actually work out?

We left the station and she got us a taxi. The driver set off like a madman, and she clutched my arm whenever the cab swung around a bend. I muttered to her, "I didn't know they drove like this in Holland." She smiled and shook her head, adding in a whisper I could barely hear, "Seems like you brought your own driver with you." I smiled and shook my head too. We kept quiet until we arrived, safe and sound.

She lived at number seven on a street with a long name I never managed to memorize. A white house, two floors, on a long terrace of similar homes that ran alongside a wide square with a quiet, peaceful garden in the middle. There was a cycle rack in front of the house. Two wide windows loomed in the facade, divided by white wooden frames. She opened the door, a little on edge, and I followed her in, also feeling nervous. She suggested I go upstairs to drop off my stuff, and then she'd show me around the place. I followed her up the narrow, wooden staircase. Hanging on the wall at the top was a framed poem in English, whose words I couldn't make out, and other pictures that seemed to be of her family. There were three rooms upstairs, and she took me into one of them, saying, "This one's *yours*." She smiled as she emphasized the possessive pronoun, and I smiled too as I looked around. She called it a room very much in the Protestant style: nothing superfluous or trivial, just a wardrobe, a bed, and a small table. She pointed out the bathroom, which she said we'd share. I smiled, saying that I didn't mind sharing, and she both smiled and blushed. She showed me what she said was the laundry room, then opened the door of the third, saying it was hers. I couldn't see a bed, but she smiled and said the bed was coming the next day, and she'd need my help moving it. I asked where she had been sleeping, and she said in the bed that was now in my room. "So that means I'm going to be sleeping in your bed? I thought we'd agreed that wasn't allowed!"

She punched me on the shoulder, then told me to relax, get changed if I wanted, and that we could either go out for dinner or make something at home.

I stopped on the way downstairs to read the poem. It was about a man looking for paradise on earth, who died as soon as he found it. He then realized that heaven and hell were the journey itself and not the end of the road. I walked down the wooden stairs, which creaked even though they were new, and found her sitting on a plush couch draped with loose white linen covers, reading the paper. She lowered the paper when she saw me, and asked if I felt refreshed, which I answered with a nod. She asked if I wanted to eat out or would rather she cooked for me. My heart jumped. Why do men feel so flattered when a woman cooks for them? Why do they feel it's an intimate gesture? I feigned surprise that she could cook, and said that would be fine as long as she tasted it first. She laughed, warning me there'd be consequences if I kept going.

She stood up and showed me around the rest of the house. There was a lounge divided into two, with armchairs overlooking the street through the window fronted by full-length linen curtains. In the other section there was a small table and four chairs. Beyond that an open, white-walled kitchen, and beyond that a small, square back garden. A door, made mainly of glass, separated the kitchen and garden, again with white linen curtains. You could see a bright little vegetable garden through the curtains. The kitchen was simple and elegant. I pulled a chair out for myself and sat watching her prepare the food. She said we'd have pasta with broccoli and olives, as long as I didn't dislike either. She started cooking, and we started talking.

I told her what had happened to me since the workshop. It was nothing that I hadn't mentioned in my emails, but she wanted to hear it from me in person. She chipped in with questions as I talked:

"What did you mean when you said you didn't like your work? Is it medicine itself, or just the hospital? How come you've done so well in this line of work? Would you be as good in a job you don't like? And how come you've stuck with this job for so many years, then? Is the problem really the type of work or is there something else you don't see, or don't want to see?"

I replied—or I gave her my usual replies.

"I'm not trying to be your shrink. I just want to understand," she continued. "What you're saying is touching, and I think I know what's worrying you, but I'm not entirely clear."

I replied to this too.

"Do you like a lot of olives in your pasta? Do you grow them in Egypt, or is it just Palestine?"

We carried on talking. She poured us a couple of glasses of port, which she said was her favorite drink. I'd never tried it before, as I preferred wine, but since it came from her hand, I loved it. It was almost midnight when she suggested we both get some sleep. I went upstairs, washed, and changed, while she cleared up a few things in the kitchen, locked the windows, and so on. I heard her come upstairs, then heard water running in the bathroom. A few minutes later she came out of the bathroom and I went out to meet her on the landing. I was wearing gray pajamas and found her wearing something similar. We both laughed and said we looked like we were on the same soccer team. The gray team! Then we said something about sleep, the morning, breakfast, and plans for tomorrow. We wished each other a good night's sleep, and she headed for her room.

At the door, I piped up: "Are you really going to make me sleep in this room?"

"Absolutely."

"But I get scared sleeping on my own."

"Don't be afraid. The house is safe."

"But I'm scared of the dark."

"There's a bedside lamp."

"But what do I do if a monster attacks me?"

"A monster?" She laughed. "If a monster comes for you, tell him I'm next door. That'll scare him off."

We swapped kisses on the cheek and went off to sleep in our separate rooms. No monster showed up.

I woke the next day to the sound of Bach from downstairs. I went down and found her sitting where she had been the day before, on the white linen couch, surrounded by newspapers. She looked up and smiled. "Did the music wake you?"

I shook my head.

She added, "I don't know why, but I like to listen to loud classical music in the morning."

I said I didn't mind as long as it was piano pieces, and not brass. She laughed and reassured me it wouldn't be. She had on black pants and a matching cotton blouse, and her hair seemed even blonder than normal. Maybe it was the sun streaming through the window onto her hair. I went over to the door leading to the garden. She said there was hot coffee in the kitchen. I poured myself a cup and went out into the garden. The weather was fresh, with a touch of cold in the air when the sun went behind a cloud. I breathed deeply and felt new oxygen coming into my lungs and waking me up. I thought to myself how pure the air seemed, my poor lungs being so used to years of Cairo pollution. I asked myself for the umpteenth time what made me stay in Cairo when I hated so much what it had become. Why did I choose to live somewhere I knew was gnawing away at my heart and soul day after day?

She put her head through the door. "Breakfast for you, sir?"

I nodded and went back in.

We had to fetch her new bed and set it up. We walked through the pretty streets of Leiden until we got to the store. They had taken her bed out of the warehouse, but the delivery guy couldn't bring it until the day after, leaving her without a bed for another night. I cajoled her into carrying it back ourselves. It wasn't far, and the bed was flat packed. We carried it through the streets, laughing at the spectacle we were making of ourselves.

"Did you know that, before a wedding, the fellaheen in Egypt parade the couple-to-be's bed around the village on a cart before they deliver it to them?"

"No I didn't. But, then again, we're not in the Egyptian countryside."

We managed, in the end, to haul the heavy bed up to her room, assemble it, and put the mattress she'd slept on the night before on top. She threw herself onto the bed to try it out, and I stood watching her, smiling quietly. Noticing me looking at her, she stood up. We went off for a stroll around Leiden's sleepy streets. She showed me around the park she'd mentioned in her emails, and said people tended to avoid it these days, but she went every day, so as not to hand it entirely over to drunks and addicts. She showed me the commercial streets that were filled with young people, and the rundown streets inhabited by immigrants and the poor. We walked along the canals that crisscrossed the town and stood on a little bridge over one of them. We passed through streets where the old buildings were: the cathedral, the town hall, the opera house, the courthouse. She told me about every building and its history. After all that, we went back to the house and carried on talking.

"You said your relationship with Salma is fraught, that she doesn't look at you when you're talking, and says nothing most of the time. How do you know it's not your fault? I know you do everything you can, but she doesn't know that. If she doesn't love you, as you suspect, whose fault is that?"

Marieke pulled no punches. She carried on: "She's only eighteen. How can the problem be hers? She's a kid, and most likely angry at you, at her mother, at the world in general. It is you who has to win her over, win her love. You say her mother's high-strung. Don't you think Salma hates her for it? And hates you for leaving her alone with her mad mother? Or maybe she thinks you're to blame for the way her mother is? In any case it must be hard for her."

I said something in reply.

"And you shouldn't give in to her mother's pigheadedness," she went on.

"Leila's out of her mind," I said. "There's no use talking to her anymore. She first turns to Sufism then ends up completely nuts. I can't make her see sense. No one can. I tried to get her dad to help, and that was a tough thing for me to do, but he got nowhere. He announced he'd given up trying to get on with her."

"And how will Salma feel if another woman comes into your life?"

I just shrugged. The subject shifted to her parents. She said her brother lived in the same town, and that he could have dinner with us if I liked. I agreed, so she called him straightaway to set it up. I was surprised at her and myself, meeting a member of her family only a day after I'd met her for the first time, in a real way, but that's what we both wanted.

I heard about Edward Said's death at the hospital. I'd never met him, but I loved him as if he were my father, and sometimes it even felt like we were the same person. Marieke used to say Said and I resembled one another in both appearance and essence. And for some reason, I had fallen headlong into a strange, unrequited, unfathomable love for someone who had never heard one word about me. And now I experienced his death as a personal loss.

The phone rang. Marieke. "Luqman, you heard what happened to Said?"

"Yes."

"I'm really sorry."

"Me too."

"Will you go to the funeral?"

"I don't know. What grounds have I got to go? They say it'll be for family only."

"Go on the grounds that he was your spiritual father."

"He didn't know that, though."

"Don't worry about that. What matters is that you go. I don't think he'd have minded. I'll go with you. Let his family kick us out if they want."

"You'll come? Really? But the funeral is before five."

"I doubt they'll miss me here. This negotiation doesn't seem like it will end anytime soon. I'll get the details of the church. Meet me in an hour at Central Park subway on Fifth. We'll go together."

What kind of strange notion made me attend the last farewell for a man who, despite having considered him my spiritual father, I had never met, accompanied by the woman I thought of as my spiritual wife, knowing well she'd never be mine? I sat on a pew among the relatives, friends, and adoring fans, listening to his loved ones lament his loss. Daniel Barenboim playing Bach, Marieke clutching and patting my arm, my heart crumbling, unstoppable tears flooding out of me. I was shaking and Marieke hugged me, warming me up and calming me a little, though tears still streamed down my face. I didn't know if I was crying for the dead, the living, or for the impossibility of our situation.

We headed for Leiden train station. She pointed out a restaurant that sold 'Egyptian food,' and one right across from it selling 'Israeli food.' They both had pictures in the window of falafel sandwiches and shawarma. She said the restaurants hadn't started fighting yet, probably because of the peace accord.

We took the train to The Hague, and sat in silence. I looked out at the green fields filled with herds of carefree cattle. We took a morning stroll past the International Court of Justice. It was cold. We stopped to take a picture in front of the court. She set the camera on automatic mode and ran to join me. I pulled her in toward me, as she held on to her black overcoat. We moved closer to one another, my shoulder brushed against her, and then I put my arm around her shoulder, a little uneasily. I didn't rest my palm on her shoulder, but clenched it, leaving it on top of her shoulder, barely touching it. We laughed, maybe at our own awkwardness, and the camera clicked. We carried on with our stroll in the peace of The Hague until we got to the main square, which was full of pigeons and a small scattering of tourists.

We had lunch in a café in the busiest part of town. The tables were scattered around the square, in between the trees and under big umbrellas. The streetlights shed a pale glow, which seemed strange on an overcast afternoon. There were very few customers, four or five at most. The waiter came over and spoke to her in Dutch, and she nodded and said, "Ja, ja. Prima." He then spoke to me and suggested what I thought must be the specials, so I nodded and copied what she had said: "Ja, ja. Prima." She held in her laughter until he had gone. She said I'd spoken at precisely the right moment in a way that made her think I'd understood what he said. We ordered food and carried on talking. She told me stories about Muslim immigrants in Holland. She said very few integrated socially. Some wanted to, but circumstances or society didn't let them. And some didn't want to integrate, trying instead to change the way society worked to fit their own ways.

We talked for a time about the meaning of the term *integration*. She said the immigrant minorities had the right to demand that the host society accommodate their customs, and to incorporate them into their way of life. But these demands aggravated those who did not want to change their ways, especially when the minority seeking them made no concessions to the host community's customs at all. We talked about the voluntary work she did in a migrant assistance center to help them negotiate the complicated healthcare system. Apologizing for interrupting our conversation, she made a couple of calls to do with the center. I heard her say "prima" several times, and started mimicking her. She scolded me as she carried on talking. Then we took a little walk around the town's main park. We laughed at her story about insisting on walking in Leiden Park to make sure ordinary citizens could keep using it. She asked me what I thought about what I'd seen so far, and I said The Hague seemed like a deserted city, at least compared to Cairo. She said that she found The Hague too quiet and conservative. We walked awhile, then sat awhile, then walked and then sat until evening came. We talked and fell silent, without the silence feeling heavy. We were silent, yet I felt we were still communicating.

At eight we arrived at an old church she said she went to some Sundays when she was in the city, and I smiled as I shook my head, faking despair.

"Really? You haven't explained this church thing yet."

"Yes I have. Dozens of times in my emails."

"You talked about it, my dear, but you haven't explained it."

"OK. I'll try and explain it, the day after tomorrow. Tomorrow we're going to Amsterdam, which is a place you don't talk about religion in. The day after, we'll go to a beach nearby to see the Atlantic. You said you've never seen the ocean before. I'll take you there, and then we'll have nothing else to do but talk."

"OK. The day after tomorrow, then."

"There's a concert by a famous cellist in this church. Pieter Wispelwey. He's going to perform pieces by your old pal Bach. Do you want to go, or do you have a problem with churches?"

"Why would I have a problem?"

"I don't know. Maybe you don't want to go into a church because you're Muslim."

"What does that have to do with it? My question to you is about faith itself, not the particular faith you follow."

"Are we going in, then?"

"So long as I don't have to pray!"

No one had to pray. Pieter Wispelwey's playing brought everyone to tears. Marieke was as happy as a child. She would glance at me from time to time, a broad smile on her face. Was she happy because we were together, because we felt so relaxed together, or was she happy to see me sitting in the middle of a church, having thought that it might be a problem? I told myself she was happy about us being together like this, right in the center of her world. We were sitting one row from the back, close together, with the rest of the audience scattered around the other wooden pews. A few glanced over at us now and again. I knew that feeling: I was the only one with dark skin in the whole church. Of course they would find it strange: what's he doing here? Is he trying to become like us? Does he show there's hope for these people? Or is he trying to fool that poor blond woman? I know this line of thinking, and I hate it. I don't want to be proof of something, a sample, or even a role model. But that night I didn't care. I smiled at the curious onlookers and filled my eyes with the beautiful Marieke, engulfed in the music crashing around the walls of the austere church. Let my soul pray, if it can, for Bach.

We left at eleven, deciding it was too late for dinner, and went back to her house and ate some fruit instead. We did our little evening dance around the sharing of the bathroom, and the kisses on the cheek. Then we each went off to sleep in our own rooms.

At exactly ten o'clock, her radiant face appeared, slowly rising up the steps from the Brooklyn Bridge subway, her bobbed blond hair blowing around her face as she approached street level. She saw me and smiled her broad, tender smile. I offered her my hand as she reached the last step. She held it and moved in closer; I hugged her. She surrendered to my embrace and we stood there hugging each other tighter and tighter. My whole body clung to hers, unwilling to let go. I didn't know that parts of my body could have independent will. I didn't know that parts of my body could long for someone, feel their touch, and calm down in their embrace in that way. It was as if my whole being implored me not to let this woman go. I didn't want to let go, and nor did she. Again, we leaned our heads back a little to see each other better, but we maintained our embrace. Her face blushed with a slight embarrassment, but she did not pull away.

We buried our faces in each other's embrace again, then looked at one another once more. Her eyes were red with tears this time, just as mine were, just as my heart was. We embraced again, not knowing what to do with ourselves. After a time—I don't know how long—we loosened our embrace a little, without relinquishing it. I put my arm around her shoulder, and she held my other arm in hers. I swallowed hard, and on we went.

We walked along the river, New York's buildings visible on the other side. People of all colors and creeds were sitting on metal benches scattered around. Japanese tourists took photographs of the New York waterfront. Others jogged, strolled, or walked their dogs. We sat. We walked. We took photos for couples and those who needed a spare hand to record their memories.

"There's no getting away from it. I love you," she said.

"And I love you," I said.

All those years hadn't passed; all that suffering hadn't happened, or no longer mattered. I, who forgive nothing, forgive you everything I suffered at your hands. She apologized for the pain she'd caused, and I said, "It's OK." She had been right. Maybe love had blinded me to the difficulties, but it hadn't stopped her from seeing them. That didn't make it her fault. I acknowledged that she had been right that our love was impossible. Neither of us could become someone else. It was love and the impossible, just like she said. She nodded.

We headed to my apartment, and she came up to see it. She had never seen where I lived before. I smiled when she said the place was just like me, and I protested that I was not that messy. She said, "Quite the opposite."

We had a glass of port together, and I lied that I had been drinking it since I'd seen her in Leiden. She laughed and said she'd given it up years ago. We spent the afternoon walking around Brooklyn, neither of us knowing how we could part, or stay together. She reminded me we had once planned to go to Venice together. Maybe we could live there, she and I, one day. We agreed on Venice as our place, in reality or as a fantasy, the place where love would triumph over the impossible, like in storybooks. It would be somewhere where the complexities of reality would lose their substance. We could spend the end of our days there. Venice—we agreed on it. I went with her to Brooklyn Bridge subway so she could catch the last train. We held each other for a long time, then parted, agreeing to meet in Central Park the day after.

Marieke took me by the hand and plunged me into Amsterdam. We hired bicycles, and I soon learned the difference between knowing how to ride a bike and navigating a city filled with thousands of them. But I stuck with it, and managed to complete the tour without getting injured. It was colder than the day before, and I didn't have the right clothes on. When I shivered she laughed at me and we went indoors to warm up. We took a glass-bottomed boat around the canals that threaded the districts of the city together. We walked a lot too, with plenty of breaks to eat, drink coffee, and warm up. And in the middle of all this, hour by hour, the reality of it all became more and more obvious to us both.

She was my soul mate. I'd never thought I'd ever say that phrase; I would have cringed to hear it, but it was true. That's how I felt, and how she felt too. Everything within us declared it. We became more at ease around each other, like two musicians who knew how to play without rehearsal. It's not what I had planned, and not what I expected. I'd hoped things would work out, but not to that extent and not that fast. I loved Marieke. Something rare happened to me in those few short days, as if a door had opened up within me and she had walked in, filling the space. It was as if she'd plunged her hand into my soul and hooked it up to hers, and then she dwelt within me.

I looked at her and knew I wasn't alone in my feelings. She was happy; a little troubled, yet happy. A broad smile rarely left her lips, putting her dimples, which I hadn't noticed before, permanently on show. Her nose and her lips blushed more. Her eyes were often heavy and sometimes tearful; at other times they were anxious, at other times straying faraway. I guessed what she was thinking, then she'd come back to me again. I knew she was like me. I was never as sure of someone's feelings as I was at that time. It was not out of hope or experience; I simply knew. I looked at her and I knew.

On the train back, she rested her head on my shoulder and slept. At Leiden station I hugged her, and we walked back to her house arm in arm. At home we hugged each other properly. On the linen-covered couch, we kissed. And we stayed on the couch until the light came through the big window, then went up to her room. We didn't wake until late the following day.

I found her awake when I opened my eyes, lying on her side of the bed, awake. She was looking intently at me. I smiled, and she smiled back. I was afraid she'd be anxious or regretful or disappointed, but her smile broadened and she stretched out a hand and stroked my face. I kissed her hand, caressed it, and ran my fingers through her short hair and the top of her neck. She rested her head on my chest.

"Good morning to you," I said.

"You ought to say good day; it's eleven thirty. I haven't slept in like that in years."

"Well the bed seems good, from what I can tell, and we put it together pretty solidly too."

She gave me a punch.

"Come on, we have to get up."

She got up, that wonderful, beautiful woman, and headed for the bathroom.

I dozed a little longer, then sensed movement in the room. She was giving me a disapproving look.

"I'm going down to make coffee, and I could use your help."

I leapt up as soon as she walked out, got washed, dressed, and descended the wooden stairs I had already grown to love. I found her at the table in the garden. We decided straightaway to put off going to the beach, as the weather was a bit dicey: it looked like it was going to rain. It was late, anyway, and the day was short. We had something light for breakfast, then went out. We went to a record shop, and I bought a few things I'd been hunting for a while. She bought me a compilation by a leading Dutch soprano, and a Bach compilation. Then we took a little walk around town. We talked about her work, and she said she wanted to leave it and do something more socially useful, like working in a public hospital or on health-insurance reform. I smiled sarcastically. "A public hospital? If only you could see the one I work at in Cairo. It's not much different from a slaughterhouse."

"That awful? Why?"

"Why? Because we have no free beds half the time, no drugs the other half, and no properly trained doctors at any time. And we have an endless flood of patients coming in that we can't treat properly. So each does what he or she wants. There are those who always try to do good, but in practice have to choose a few to treat, and write off the rest. There are those who try to be fair and spread the resources around as evenly as possible, even if all the patients end up worse off. And there are those who don't care and try to do as little as they can, even if it means patients die. And then there are trainees who use these patients to practice on, especially when the lack of qualified doctors means they aren't supervised often enough. They learn by trial and error."

"That's terrible."

"Yes, it is."

"How can you live with it? How long have you put up with it?"

"Seven years."

She went quiet when I told her that. Her eyes filled with tears, and she hugged me. I told her not to worry, that I was used to it, that it was nothing dramatic. But she kept on hugging me, saying it was awful, and asking how I could have put up with it all those years. I don't know what happened after that exactly, but I felt a lump in my throat, and I started silently crying. Then it turned into sobbing, and she hugged me closer. We were sitting on an old stone wall near a little canal bridge. I had my head buried in her lap, my body shivering now and then. I don't know how long it took for me to calm down. I stayed silent for a time, then I said she'd have to go home and get changed because I'd made her sweater all wet. She laughed, and so did I; she kissed me, and we headed back to the house.

She asked me why I had held all my emotions in like that for so long, and why I didn't hate my work because of all that I'd seen. I tried to explain:

"What else can I do? If I let my emotions take over, I wouldn't last long in Egypt. Everything is the same over there, more or less. Different kinds of things, but the same logic. People die in hospitals, sometimes from direct negligence that you can see with your own eyes. But what about the other kinds of negligence you don't see, and that kills thousands? What would you do if you knew about it, if you could see it too?"

She shook her head in sorrow, and said, "I don't know. How could I know? I read about this stuff. I listen to you, and to others, but it seems to me beyond ordinary people's capacity to deal with. You don't know how much I respect people who live in those circumstances. I don't pity them; I respect them. I see them as special, above and beyond normal humanity. Do you know what first attracted me to you? You seemed aware of human tragedy, yet were still optimistic. Your sense of humor mixes this sharp sense of tragedy with a lust for life. I don't know how you do it. I don't think I could."

"It's simple. There's nothing great about it at all. You grow up and find yourself living under a brutal system that crushes people. And when it crushes you the first time, you scream in pain, but you have to get up and walk, even if it's on one leg. Humans can cope with the worst conditions. You try to finish the day you started. What else can you do?"

"I don't know. It's all beyond me. I've lived my whole life here, between Leiden, The Hague, and Amsterdam. Even when I've traveled, it's been to Paris or Germany or some-where like that. Then to New York, which feels like quite an adventure. I'm lucky. Everything I know about human trag-edy is from others: from you, from the immigrants I meet, from books, from TV. I'm a child of luxury; I can't claim the right to judge these things."

"You're an extremely clever woman. And you have a tre-mendous ability to see right into people, to understand their thinking, to understand the spirit behind that way of thinking. I've never met anyone like you before in that way."

I was being completely sincere. She smiled and said calmly, but completely seriously, "I could say exactly the same about you. I can hardly believe what's happening to me. I can't believe I've found this degree of connection with another person, with a person from a completely different world who nonetheless feels like my other half."

She fell silent and brushed away her tears, so I hugged her. She laughed embarrassedly. "Is it my turn to soak your coat now?"

We laughed, and walked arm in arm along the canal toward the restaurant where we were to meet her brother.

I was dreading it. We walked in and I followed her toward a young man, who she kissed. He was even blonder than her, polite, but distant. His eyes didn't give himself away, as if he were looking at you through glass. We swapped small talk: about Holland, Egypt, and other trivialities people resort to when they have nothing to really talk about. He mentioned something about his studies, and asked me about my work. Marieke wanted to know about his girlfriend, and he replied that she had gone traveling, and that things were shaky between them. We were all quiet for a while; then he asked my view on what was happening in the Middle East. I smiled and replied between bites of bread that I didn't know what he was talking about exactly, because I hadn't followed the news for a few days. Marieke blushed and looked reproachfully at me. He said there had been some violence in the West Bank. People had been killed the last three days in a row. It was the beginning of October, and I really hadn't heard or seen any news since I'd arrived. He asked me what I thought could be done to resolve the conflict, and the way the conversation was turning started to make me feel uncomfortable. I tried to cut it short, but he seemed compelled to pursue it. He told me he thought the Arabs had made a mistake in opposing Jewish migration to Palestine in the last century. If they had done like the Dutch, and welcomed the oppressed, they would have avoided this conflict altogether. I said something about there being a difference between the Huguenots seeking refuge from repression and Zionists seeking a place they could evict people from and settle. We differed, of course, on the history of it all. He said he understood how strongly I felt, being a Palestinian. Marieke interrupted, a little annoyed, and reminded him I was Egyptian. He was quiet for a while, then started up again. I felt more and more suffocated. I smiled and joked with him about the accuracy of our historical knowledge, then suggested we go to Marieke's and watch the news to find out who'd been the killer that day. He apologized, saying he had another engagement. We stood, shook hands, and he left, while Marieke and I went back to number seven.

I sat in front of the TV, and Marieke came in to pour two glasses of port. The news started and I saw what had been going on in the Palestinian Territories since September 28. There appeared on the screen a man with a child, about eleven or twelve years old, sitting in the street behind a concrete block that provided them with inadequate cover. The sound of gunfire was endless, and the man was hiding behind the concrete block, sheltering the boy behind him and, at the same time, trying to point out to the shooters that he had a child with him. The scene lasted a few seconds, and apparently my voice was rising, because Marieke rushed in to hear me screaming "My God!" just at the moment the child was killed in the arms of the man, who slumped down on top of him. A rigid silence came over me. She sat next to me and hugged me, but I did not cry. I just kept staring at the TV in silence. She reached over and turned it off. I sat there, unmoving. We were quiet for the rest of the evening.

We met the following day as agreed, and walked around Central Park a little. Then I took her to Bergdorf Goodman.

"I want to buy you something."

"What's the occasion?"

"Just because I've never bought you anything, and I want to."

"From Bergdorf's? How much is that hospital paying you?"

"It doesn't matter, I'll buy you something small."

I bought her a six-hundred-dollar woolen hat, which we both realized was ridiculous, and then we went and had a sumptuous meal at a new restaurant in the Meatpacking District. Afterward, we walked for quite a while, as far as the Rockefeller Center, where we looked around at a whimsical art exhibition. All day, we walked around arm in arm, or hand in hand, or with one of our hands clutching the other, or my arm over her shoulder, or her head on my shoulder, or her arm around my waist. We spent the day in each other's embrace, as if making up for all the time we'd missed out on, or for all the time that was to come. Why did we do that to each other, Marieke?

I woke up late the following day; she wasn't in bed. I washed and went down in my gray pajamas, and found her in the kitchen. I said good morning, and she told me the coffee was ready. She'd woken up early, so had fetched some newspapers in English for me to read. I smiled and thanked her. I kissed her on the back of the neck, and sat sipping coffee and reading. The pictures of Muhammad al-Durra, the boy I'd seen killed onscreen the day before, covered the pages. Marieke said it was a conservative paper, which didn't normally print graphic pictures like that.

We talked about it a little, then went off to visit Scheveningen, a coastal town nearby. It was fairly sunny, and we walked around in the peace and quiet. We talked about yesterday: what had happened in the Occupied Territories. She clutched my arm and told me how sad she felt when she saw such things, and how it broke her heart to see the cruelty of human beings and the stupidity that made them go out and kill. On the bus, she sat wrapped in my arms, and we watched the scenery go by. She asked me how I felt about it, and how I dealt with it. I shrugged and said I didn't deal with it. I saw it just like I saw my work at the hospital, like the polluted air I inhaled.

"I often ask myself why I don't emigrate. But I only ask; I never come up with an answer. And I also know I'll never do it."

"I know."

"How?"

"Because if you emigrated, you wouldn't be the same person."

"I normally cannot explain that to anyone."

"You don't need to. I can feel it. I think anyone who really knows you, knows you couldn't settle outside Egypt."

We'd come to the beach. The gentle waves rolled on the long, sandy shoreline. There were little white sand dunes topped with tufts of grass and nothing much else. It was overcast, threatening rain, and there was a breeze blowing. We walked along the beach wrapped up in all manner of clothes: she with a red woolen scarf around her neck, her glasses perched high on her forehead, her face having taken on a very serious expression.

She told me about her faith. Jesus was not, for her, someone who lived two thousand years ago. "Maybe he did, or he didn't. It makes no difference to me. He's an idea. An idea of tolerance and sacrifice, that humans shouldn't hurt their sisters and brothers. He's an idea of love between people. God's in my heart. He's the light that shows me the way. I don't need proof or rationales. It's not about proving His existence or not. It's about going deep into your heart and finding something pure that guides you down the right and true path. It's a light that's within you, me, and everybody. That's what it is to me."

"And what about the church itself? And rituals?"

"The church is the assembly point, bringing people together. It's the link that joins me to the rest of the people in Leiden who share my convictions. We're not a traditional church and, don't forget, we're Protestants. I believe each individual has a direct connection to God. I don't need intermediaries, but we do need a church that brings us together to do good, to cement our solidarity. You know, most of our meetings are about worldly things, like looking after the park I told you about, or helping those in need, the poor, the immigrants, improving the city and the way we go about things, even the spiritual troubles we encounter. It's a solidarity network."

"I have to say that the more you tell me about it the more it puts me off. Don't you feel it's all a bit fake? A church that isn't founded on religious conviction sounds more like a group-therapy network. Or a town council. Why talk about these things in a religious institution? Aren't there charities, town halls, political parties? It seems like some kind of underground sect."

"It's not a sect and it's not underground. It's a church, and it's open to all. Yes, there are all these institutions, but we are a spiritual union. There are spiritual and religious ties between us that enable us to work in the institutions you talk about."

"I still don't get this idea of spiritual religion. Do you believe in, you know, a God who created the earth in seven days, in heaven and hell and salvation and all that stuff?"

"Many of us don't believe those things, but the spiritual union that unites is something stronger than traditional Christianity."

The rain had begun to pelt us, and I joked that God was punishing us for heresy, but she didn't find it funny. We hid in

110

a small, almost-deserted restaurant, and she carried on trying to explain her faith and her connection to her church, but I could not get it. I declared defeat, but she wouldn't accept it, saying it was an important issue to her. She needed me to understand it properly. We took a break while we ate, and then she started again, and pursued the subject all the way home. I couldn't work out how a liberal doctor in Holland could be open to this religious stuff. And she couldn't understand how I could turn away from my soul in such a way.

We both had work to do all day, but we met for an hour at lunchtime. We didn't eat. She took me by the hand and led me to Third Avenue. She reminded me I needed a briefcase, something we'd talked about by email a year ago. She decided to take me to a place she knew to buy one. She told me about the different types of leather, and recommended what she said was a famous brand. I narrowed it down to two, and left the final choice to her. She bought me the brown one. She asked me if I had bought Salma anything, and I shook my head and said she had more than enough bags already. She laughed and said I really was a fool if I thought there was such a thing as enough when it came to girls and bags. She chose one I would never have bought, and then we went back out. It was two o'clock and we both had to get back to work, but we didn't want to part. Finally, we steeled ourselves to do it, joked with each other how we were behaving like teenagers, and headed off for the subway.

We went back to her house, where I packed quickly, and then headed for the train station to start my trip back. We planned to grab something to eat at a place near the station; I suggested the Israeli restaurant. I wanted to know what this Israeli food was all about: it looked the same as our shawarma and falafel. When we went in she did the talking so that they wouldn't pick up on my enemy accent. The waiter sounded one hundred percent Egyptian to me. She laughed when I told her, and asked how I could tell when he was speaking Dutch. I swore he was Egyptian. When he came with the food, I spoke to him in Egyptian Arabic:

"Do you make falafel with fuul or chickpeas?"

"Just chickpeas, sir. It's hard to find fuul round here."

"Whose place is this?"

"It belongs to me and a group of friends."

"What this 'Israeli food' stuff about then?"

"Some Israeli used to own it, but we bought it and found the Dutch like the Israeli food story, so we kept it that way. But we're all Egyptians."

"Well, can we have some tahina then?"

She fell about laughing when I translated the gist of the conversation for her. We ate our "Israeli food" and headed for the station. We sat waiting for the train. We got lost in conversation, lost track of time, and still hadn't gotten to the important things: when would we meet again? *Would* we meet again? What did all that mean? We'd acted like a couple who knew they'd be together, yet my train was coming and I was going to get on it and she'd stay behind. We'd decided nothing, but we acted as if we everything was sorted out. I loved her, she loved me, and we both felt embarrassed we'd fallen in love so quickly. Would she come and live with me in Cairo, when she'd only seen the Third World on the news? Or would I try and send myself into exile, knowing I never could?

There was an hour or so until my train. We sat in a large pavement café with wooden seats like those in downtown Cairo, and ordered hot chocolate. I told her I wanted to see her again soon, and she agreed. I decided to be Dutch, if only for an hour, and asked her if she wanted to come and live with me in Cairo. She blushed and said she wanted to try it, but she wasn't sure it was a good idea, the right time, the circumstances: that kind of thing. I suggested that she try it out—that we try it out. Why not come at Christmas and spend a few months with me? I laughed genuinely for the first time that day, and held her in my arms on the platform for a long time. We parted with her agreeing to come and stay with me at Christmas.

She asked me what I would do that evening, after she caught her flight. I said it was Salma's birthday, and she was coming in from DC that evening for a get-together. Her mother—Salma's remote controller—insisted that the birthday party be at Darwish's, not at my place or at a restaurant, or any other public place. He also had to be in charge of the invitations, and had invited her veiled aunt Amira and her weird husband, Daoud. The directives issued to Darwish were too many for his taste: he was more used to giving orders than receiving them. So he went ahead and invited everyone who knew Salma, one way or another, from far and wide, in effect ruining my daughter's twenty-first. Maybe that's what Leila wanted. If she wasn't going to be there, there was no need for a proper birthday party. Nothing new in that.

Marieke looked at me for a long time, then snapped: "And why do you accept this?"

We talked it over at length, like we did that day in Leiden. I said many things, and she said many things, though she was quite tough about it. She said there was a difference between respecting the demands of others and being passive. The word kept echoing around in my head: *passive*. She asked me if I'd meet Salma at the station, and I said wasn't sure yet. She shook her head in reproach and said, "Don't you see? That's passivity. Why not meet her at the station with some flowers or a gift of some kind and take her to the house in a taxi? Or walk there together? It'll give you a chance to talk to her before the others show up."

I wanted to protest at her calling me passive, but we didn't have much time left: Marieke was leaving that evening. So I said maybe I would go and meet Salma at the station and I asked her if I had to see her off at the station as well. She smiled, but didn't reply.

I took the day off, and Marieke did the same. We met for the last time at Brooklyn Bridge station. We walked and talked about everything, then reached the same point we always did. She said, "I can't live in Egypt. I can't live outside Holland really. Maybe not even outside Leiden. That's how I am. I've realized that's how I am, attached to this plot of earth, to my people here and my community. And to the church you sneer at. Maybe New York."

I laughed and reminded her that New York used to be called New Amsterdam, and that her forefathers had built it, so it wasn't really an exception to her rule. She asked me seriously if I thought I could live in New York forever.

I asked how love could be limited by geography.

She got angry and said, "It's not love that's limited; it's the chance of being able to live together that is."

I shrugged off the idea. "And where would that leave Egypt then?"

She said, "I know."

We fell silent.

Why didn't we try? Even if we failed, we'd cure ourselves of this love that would not leave us alone. Or maybe we didn't want to be cured. We talked about us once again. Everything we said, we'd said before. We came to no conclusion we hadn't reached before. Time passed, and her train was getting closer.

She said, "Maybe we'll meet in old age, toward the end. Maybe in another time, another era."

I looked at her, but did not reply. Was this the passivity she talked about?

She took the woolen hat I'd bought her out of her bag and put it on. She got her camera ready. I held the bag she had bought me over my shoulder so that it would be in the picture. We each took a picture of the other, then took the last one of the two of us together.

6

John Quincy Adams Elementary

WASHINGTON WAS HOT. ADNAN TOOK off his raincoat and stood there in his shirt, but it was no use. The humidity made it hard to breathe. This was not the best time to go looking for memories, but it was the only time he had. He only had a few hours left in DC.

He had arrived the evening before, spent the morning sorting out a few legal matters, and then went off to look for his old home. He'd come here after that. He'd taken the Metro to Dupont Circle and walked the rest of the way, just like his mother used to do when she walked him to school. He hadn't been back to DC since he'd left school, and everything he remembered about it was mixed up and muddled. He'd turned the page on all that some time ago. He thought he'd left it behind when he went to university in Detroit and settled there. Twenty years had passed since then, during which time his whole life had changed, but when the opportunity presented itself, he'd come back to cast an eye over the old places and to visit his old elementary school.

Adnan was dripping with sweat. He was looking for John Quincy Adams Elementary on foot. It was around here somewhere. He'd checked online that morning at the hotel, and made sure of the address: 2020 Nineteenth Street NW, in Adams-Morgan. The website had also mentioned that the neighborhood was not, like many thought, named after one person, but after its two elementary schools. Until desegregation,

John Quincy Adams Elementary had been for white kids, and Thomas P. Morgan Elementary had been for "colored" kids. Adnan hadn't known that. He thought to himself that it was ironic that he had gone to JQA, when it seemed he'd really belonged at Morgan. His father must have given the school a false address in the school district, but he never knew what made him send him to this school when they'd lived in Virginia.

There was Nineteenth Street. The street rose up slightly as you approached the school: he remembered that. And there was the school beckoning in the distance. That had to be it. He looked around and peered down toward the end of the street. There was no other building that could be a school. Yes, that had to be it, but it seemed bigger than he remembered. Strange: things normally looked smaller.

He approached the school and went slowly up the wide marble steps. Even the doors seemed bigger. He went through them and looked around. He went over to the desk and explained to the receptionist that he was a former pupil and wanted to have a look around. She seemed accustomed to this sort of thing—people coming to look back on their old lives—and said she would make an exception for him as it was during the vacation, so long as he was quick.

He went through the door and walked the long corridor parallel to the classrooms until he got to the other staircase. It had small, narrow steps where the bullies used to set up their ambushes for unfortunates like him. This was where the torture happened, maybe once a week. On the rare occasions he had money on him, he'd be stripped of it. But the bullies always took his food, sneering at him in disgust as they asked him the name of that "mush" his mother had made him. The first time, he'd replied that it was called "fuul." He'd said it in Arabic because he didn't know what to call it in English. The other boys couldn't believe it, and roared with laughter. One of them tried some, then spat it out. They sniffed and passed around half a Saran-wrapped pita, laughing their heads off, then tore it to shreds in front of him as he stood powerlessly looking on. From that day onward, that became his nickname in school: "Fool."

He did one more round of the corridors, then left. He stood in front of the doors for a few moments. Was this it? He'd decided to come after a long battle with himself, over whether it was better just to leave the past where it was and forget about it. He'd thought long and hard over it, and had even read about what it meant to revisit your past in a book on psychology, and after much doubting and debating with himself, he decided to come. He wanted to summon the person he once was—an eight-, ten-, twelve-year-old kid—but he felt nothing. No flood of emotions, no tears. His sole focus was on trying to remember: was that really the corridor he'd preserved in his memory? Was that really the staircase he'd feared passing every day, the one where the bullies would humiliate him? He'd definitely come to the right place; this was John Quincy Adams Elementary, that's what the sign said. Yet still he felt nothing except the stifling humidity.

He had gone there every school day, all those years ago. His dad would bring him in his funny '74 Chevy Impala. Where had his father even found that old wreck of a luxury car? He had driven it for as long as Adnan had been conscious of the world. He was proud of how big it was: "Twenty feet long," he'd keep saying. Adnan had measured it once, found that it was in fact only two hundred and twenty-three inches long, and rushed back into the house to tell his dad. His dad was eating something: soup, as he recalled. His father's face had suddenly turned red, and he threw his spoon at Adnan. He remembered clearly the splatters of soup flying through the air as the spoon hurtled toward his face, but it missed and hit the TV screen instead. That made him even madder. He stood up to grab Adnan, but his mother stepped in, allowing him a few precious seconds to make his escape. He couldn't remember how that episode had ended. He must have apologized to his dad; his mom must have asked him to, and he must have done so to ward off worse consequences. It all ended peacefully, but he learned that day not to say anything critical about the Impala.

His dad had owned lots of cars, six or seven. He had opened a car-rental office when Adnan was in fourth grade, and they made up its fleet. He remembered the day he opened the office, as his mom, unusually, had taken him to school instead of his dad. It had been a milestone for the family: his father had turned from a driver into a boss. In the beginning, that didn't change much in Adnan's life, except that his mom took him to school more often: once or twice a week maybe. He loved that. His mother would take him on the Metro to Dupont Circle. He was dazzled by the shiny Metro railcars and the platform's flashing lights as the train entered the station. He was amazed trains could travel so fast and so freely underground. He remembered his astonishment when he first walked out of Dupont Circle: the elongated escalators that took so long to get to the top. He hadn't known that he and all these other people had been so far below street level. He loved everything about his journey to school and back with his mom: holding her hand the whole time, clinging to her, the pastries she used to feed him, her patience as she stood and waited for him when he stopped dead, something having caught his eye. She'd stop, and together they'd look at whatever it was.

She never worried about being late for school—the opposite of his dad, who always rushed him. With his mother he sometimes had to remind her to speed up. It was as if they were going to a picnic. They'd contemplate the many different faces they saw in the railcars. He'd point things out to her, and she'd hush him, with a conspiratorial smirk on her face. He'd laugh and bury his head in her lap while she stroked his hair.

The Impala was very wide, and the front seat was a long, door-to-door couch. He'd always slide around at the many bends in the road, especially as his dad took them too fast. He'd start off clutching the door and watching the streets, the traffic lights, the street signs, and all the different types of cars. Then the car would suddenly take a corner too quickly and he'd slide all the way over to his dad, whose fiery look would command him to sit still. Adnan would crawl back to the door handle and into the world of his thoughts. He'd try to hang on to it, but his mind would wander again until the car took another sharp bend, and so it would go on. It was this—the fast driving, the over-large front seat, and the fear of provoking his father's anger—that would preoccupy him, along with a feeling of nausea he had whenever he was in the Impala. He didn't dare tell his father about this nausea. He did tell his mom, who told him that everyone got carsick. It was bit like seasickness, she told him. He didn't know what seasickness meant, so he kept quiet. He'd get in the car early every morning, still half asleep, dreading the impending nausea, trying to fight it off, hanging on to the door, teeth clenched and face pale. If his dad spoke to him, he'd mumble some words that would wear down his father's patience as he returned his focus to the road, shaking his head in despair. Adnan would withdraw into himself again and try to hold himself steady.

At every intersection Adnan would look in the direction they weren't taking, hoping in his heart that his dad would go that way rather than along the familiar route. He knew the usual route they took, and didn't want to go where it took them. He dreamed of seeing some different scenery. He once asked his dad where some other street led to; his dad looked at him with scorn and said that it went to somewhere they weren't going. He remembered this, and wondered about that street. He couldn't remember its name, but he'd never gone down there when he was a kid. Or maybe he had, later on, not knowing it was one of the streets he'd longed to explore as the Impala had speeded past.

He went down the steps to the sidewalk in front of the school, and walked uphill looking for the little park. After a few minutes, its iron railings loomed into sight. To save time by avoiding a U-turn on Columbia Street, his father would drop him off on the corner, and Adnan had crossed the park every day to get to the school gates. He gazed around anxiously and wondered why it seemed so different. The playing field in the middle was still the same. The steep hill was just as hard to climb. But it seemed different. Perhaps he was looking at it from the wrong angle. Had that building always been there, and was that a public toilet or a park-keeper's cabin? Maybe there was another park on the other side.

A tall, dark-skinned woman entered the park from the other side and sat next to the small building he didn't recognize. He thought about going over to ask her, but changed his mind. What would he say? He looked over at her again. From this distance she looked like a girl he'd been in school with. One of the bullies said she was an Indian, so they all started joking about her wearing feathers and carrying arrows. They laughed about it, but one of the more studious girls, sneering at her classmates' ignorance, pointed out that the girl was an Indian from India, not a Red Indian. The roughest of the bullies dismissed the distinction: "Aren't they all Indians?" From that time on, she became the "red girl." Adnan liked the "red girl," but never dared to speak to her. She was the target of ridicule too, and he didn't want to make it worse for himself by being seen with her. Could that be her now, sitting at the far end of the park? He peered over at her. She'd taken out a handkerchief and was wiping her face. Was she crying? No, it must be the heat and humidity. A tall, dark-skinned woman sitting in a park was not exactly unusual—she could be anyone, even if she looked the same age as the red girl would have been.

"Forget all this and leave the woman alone," he told himself.

The heat was stifling. He realized the clothes he had on were totally inappropriate. He'd come in from Detroit, and it hadn't occurred to him that the weather in DC would be like this. He smiled to himself. "You never wear the right stuff. You never did when you were a kid and you don't now that you're forty. And now it's your own fault, for sure."

It all came back to him in a flash of pain: being a kid always in the wrong clothes. He never wore the right things for the winter cold or the summer heat; he never wore the right clothes when school was out, or for the few birthday parties he was invited to. The shame was like a burden you bore and you didn't want anyone else to see. You tried to hide it by hiding yourself. You tried to take up less space, to keep out of the other kids' line of sight. In class, you sat at a side desk: not at the front with the keen kids, not at the back with the tough guys, but in the middle where no one would notice you. In the schoolyard, at parties, you went to the farthest corner and kept as quiet as you could. If you met anyone, or someone spoke to you, you wrapped up the conversation as quickly as you could. Staying silent was not guaranteed to work, though; it might attract more stares and intensify your yearning to disappear. Adnan always wondered where his parents had bought his clothes; it certainly wasn't where the rest of his classmates got theirs. He saw a pair of jeans in a store near his dad's office once, the kind the cool kids wore. He got up the courage to ask his dad to buy them for him, but his dad just bawled him out for being selfish and greedy and making endless demands. He never asked for anything like that again. His clothes weren't right, nor were his school supplies or his toys.

He decided to stop thinking about this stuff, or he'd never get out of DC. He couldn't carry on reminiscing about his toys, and the ragging he got for it all through his childhood; the ski gear he'd worn to this park one day that made him the laughing stock of his classmates; the hats and gloves that were either too big or too small for him. He never had a girlfriend that whole time, or any friends at all for that matter. Everyone kept their distance.

He looked around the park again. Was this really where he'd come every day? After school, he'd wait for his dad again.

Another trip in the Impala. He used to both love and hate this journey. He loved it because it took him to the comfort of home, to the care, cooking, and spoiling of his mom. He hated it because the Impala would be too hot in summer and too cold in winter. His dad didn't like using the AC when they stopped at the lights; he wasn't sure why. His dad told him it wore out the engine, but Adnan thought that odd. Why had Chevrolet designed it in such a dumb way? Didn't they know there were traffic lights in America? He asked his dad these questions and was silenced by a stream of abuse. That was before the Impala-measuring incident. From then on, he surrendered to the vagaries of temperature in the car on the way home. That distracted him from thinking about his overpowering nausea. He managed to steal some sleep sometimes, at the price of a telling-off from his dad when they arrived home.

Dad would fall asleep after a late lunch, and his mother would impose a kind of shutdown on the little house: no moving, no talking. Adnan would end up falling asleep too, and by the time he woke up his dad would already be gone, back at work until ten at night. Adnan would make sure to sneak off to bed before his dad got home, filling the house with cursing about the cabdrivers or customer holdups or a neighbor who had parked in his favorite spot or a quarterly bank bill or—if none of the above were available—whatever or whoever he laid eyes on first at home. To avoid any of this, Adnan would give up whatever he'd be watching on TV, sneak off to bed at nine fifty-five exactly, and wait anxiously. His heart would sink as he heard the heavy engine coming to a stop under his window, then the five wooden steps of the porch creaking under his dad's huge frame, and then the key in the lock, followed by the cursing.

There were also the evenings spent in his father's office during vacations. Adnan had always tried to get out of it, but never managed to. His dad would say something about a son helping his father out, that he ate and drank all year at his expense, and that it wouldn't kill him to do a few things around the office for his old pop in return. Answer the phone, for example. He hated going to the office with his dad, but it wasn't all bad: there was Sunita, the girl of Indian descent, at the reception desk. She often came to work in a colorful sari. The prettiest thing about that, in Adnan's eyes, was that you could see her whole midriff—her stomach, her spine, her waist. He could sit looking at her freely, especially when his dad wasn't around. The line of her belly changed whenever she leaned one way or shifted her stance. He got to know everything about her, and sought her out. She was the main attraction at that stage of his life, she and the cheese Pringles he managed to sneak whenever he earned a dollar here or there.

He also loved to listen to Abu Zuhdi, the Palestinian cab-driver who told amusing tales about Egypt, Palestine, and other countries he claimed to have lived in. He told stories about Adnan's father too, and encouraged him not to take slaps and insults from him like that without giving it back. Adnan was perplexed by what Abu Zuhdi had suggested. How could he "give it back"? He'd only get more abuse if he did, and maybe a whipping with the rope or the belt, like he'd got-ten the year before when he refused to go to the office. Even worse, it would mean days of dreadful silence throughout the house, and his mother would suffer too. Abu Zuhdi said a lot of things that Adnan did not really understand, though he did love to listen to him.

The truth was that there were other sources of amusement at the office even when his dad was there, like the grilled chicken, pickled cucumber, and Lebanese bread they had some evenings, or the fuul and hummus Abu Zuhdi made on weekend morn-ings (since Adnan's father didn't believe in the idea of weekends off). Then again, nights at the office meant fewer chances to spend the evening with his mom and the TV, and more chance of being the victim of his father's sudden fits of rage.

Adnan realized, standing looking at the park, that every moment of his childhood was a mixture of love and hatred, joy mingled with misery. It surprised him that he had never seen it that way before. When he left the family home to go to university in Detroit, he was both angry and suffocated by his father's authoritarianism. His anger at his father exploded when his mother died, two years after he had gone to college. His father had her buried before informing his absent son of her death. He justified it by saying that a body should be buried as soon as possible, according to Islamic law and custom. For Adnan, it was the last straw, or maybe a chance to do what he had secretly longed to do throughout his whole childhood. He didn't take his father on, he just thanked him for letting him know and hung up. He never spoke to his father again, nor did his father try to contact him. Adnan was quite amazed not to hear from him, but relieved not to have to confront him, which he had been dreading. His decision to cut his father off was vindicated and their relationship ended in silence.

His father had died two months ago. Adnan hadn't gone to the funeral. Revenge. He decided to return the favor to his dead old man, and dumped the ceremony on some Muslim charity or other to sort out, and hired a lawyer to dispose of his father's estate. He hadn't been back to DC until the day before, after his mother's uncle Darwish invited him to Salma's birthday party in New York. He was touched by the invite, and decided to go to DC first to tie up a few matters, then on to New York to see Salma. He hadn't known she was in New York. He hadn't seen Salma or her mother since the summer vacations when they were kids. Adnan had loved Darwish ever since he was a kid. He remembered their visits to his house, and how they pleased his mother. Maybe he loved Darwish for that reason, because he couldn't recall him having been particularly kind to him. Maybe he gave him a gift once: probably a book. He couldn't exactly remember. He'd loved him because his mother had loved him. She used to say she was so proud that her uncle was such a great man, and wanted Adnan to grow up and be like him.

More importantly, though, these visits to Darwish's were a chance to meet up with Leila. She and Adnan were around the same age, but she was gutsier. It was she who first tried to make friends, and took him on walks to see her "secret places" around New York. There was nothing special about them: a hot dog cart, a burger bar, a coffee shop, a juice bar, a place on the river under a bridge (he couldn't remember where). She'd talk all the time, and he would listen, fascinated more than anything else. She talked about life and school in Egypt, the boys and girls, as if she were revealing a magical world to him: a world where the boys all had names and faces like his, and habits and clothes like his. He told her he'd love to go to a school like the one she described in Egypt, and she replied that if he did he'd be the star of the playground, because he'd have come from America.

He fantasized about that for a long time: being the star of the school. He didn't see Leila for another two or three years: he couldn't remember how long exactly. She had grown up, but was still as impulsive as ever. They quickly rekindled their friendship; by that time he had become a little more talkative. When he saw her next, he was with his mother and it was during a short visit to New York. He'd left school and was about to move to Detroit for college, and she'd moved to live with her father after her mother had died. They would make a good match, his mother told him after she had hugged Leila and looked her up and down. Leila was dressed all in black and seemed full of sadness. He realized he'd loved her since that first summer he'd met her, but he hadn't had the courage to come out with it, and when she said he should write her from Detroit, he timidly nodded, but knew he wouldn't.

Adnan didn't keep in touch with Professor Darwish much after he left his family home in Washington. He didn't write to Leila, of course, because she doubtless had many admirers in New York. She wouldn't bother herself with a guy like him. He used to send Professor Darwish a birthday card, however, as his mother had asked him to, and he carried on doing so even after she died. Adnan had stopped off in New York once or twice over the years, and had visited Darwish. By chance, he met Salma there both times. His heart jumped when he saw her the first time. She looked so like Leila, her mother, when she was young, at least as far as he could remember. Leila wasn't there either time he visited and met Salma, thank God, yet he felt a strange kind of fatherly affection for her daughter. Then he lost track of her, and she stopped visiting Darwish. So Adnan was surprised when Darwish got in contact to invite him to Salma's birthday party. He wondered what he should he bring and whether Leila would be there too. He didn't dare ask Darwish. He'd find out that night when he got to New York.

Adnan had arrived in Washington the evening before, signed a few papers, and dealt with the last of his father's affairs that morning. He'd then decided to cast a glance over his past: the school, the house. He'd spent an hour looking for the house, until an old lady told him they had knocked the whole block down and built a new apartment complex. Condos. He looked at them and felt nothing. There was nothing even remotely resembling the home he remembered. Even the way the street looked had changed. He didn't waste much time there, and went looking for the school, and now here he was: John Quincy Adams Elementary.

Here, in front of this park, he had waited every day for his father after school. His father was always late. Adnan couldn't remember ever coming out of class and finding him there. Sometimes he was so late Adnan would be left alone in the park, the last of the kids to leave. He would pretend the park was the grounds of his palace, and that he was one of those pashas his mother said were her forebears. He would run around the park, surveying his domain, ordering the peasants around and whipping them. Sometimes the metal animal statues played the role of the suffering peasants beaten into mute submission. He did it all to pretend he wasn't afraid or unnerved by his solitude in the park, but fear always overcame him in the end and he'd withdraw into a corner with his imaginary whip and curl up there until he heard the engine of the ancient Impala. He'd briefly rejoice and run toward the car, but then come up against the towering figure of his father, with his fierce expression. He'd get into the Impala, hang on tightly to the door, and try not to provoke his father's anger.

He thought about how his father could make him feel both safe and afraid at the same time. His father's arrival would expel one kind of fear and replace it with another. The first type of fear was nebulous, because he didn't know what exactly he was afraid of: being abducted or left on the street with no way home. They were evils of unknown consequence.

The janitor came into the park once and found him hunkered down in a corner. School was long over and the staff and pupils had all gone. The street was completely empty. The janitor stopped, got off his bike, and said something to Adnan he didn't understand. He seemed nice, but he had a strong accent Adnan couldn't make out. Then he realized he'd asked him to get on the bike with him. He hesitated at first, but then did so. He didn't know where the janitor would take him, since he didn't even know his own address, but he didn't know what to do other than obey the man. But then the Impala appeared and it all ended well. Adnan avoided the janitor after that, asking himself whether he'd planned to kidnap him. (Of course, his father scolded him severely for getting on the bike with the janitor.) His father showing up dispelled one set of fears, but put others in their place: fear his dad would suddenly turn red, spin around, and slap him across the face, or intimidate him in some other way with threats of the belt or broken bones, or, even worse, that he'd carry them out on his mother.

His loathing for his father raged within him at times like those. He imagined taking hold of his father's broad shoulders and shoving him up against a wall, or pushing him out of his speeding car. He wished from the bottom of his heart that his dad would disappear: die suddenly, shrivel up to nothing, evaporate, crash the Impala, or fall down the deep ravine they passed over every morning. Sometimes he imagined grabbing the wheel and steering it down into the ravine. Of course he never did anything. He just kept quiet; then his mother would ask him to apologize, which he would; and then his father would forgive him, though he never knew what he'd done wrong.

Over time, his main aim around his father became to avoid sparking his anger. He even learned a few tricks to win his father's praise: a word or two to back up what his dad said, a compliment either for his dad or the Impala, and a great deal of smiling. He did it to win his father's praise and avoid his wrath, but then he started to use these ruses to achieve concrete goals, like a night in with his mother and the TV, or a dollar to buy the banned Pringles, or something even greater: getting a wristwatch for his eleventh birthday. His ability to get around his father got better with practice. He learned to mention things to his mother, while his dad took his after-noon nap—things he knew his father would hear through his light sleep. He perfected this art, and once told his mom how guilty he felt that his father worked so hard all the time, for his benefit, and that he hoped to grow up one day and repay his father for all the good he'd done for him. That one got him the watch, yet it still felt like something of a defeat.

It was getting hotter. These clothes really weren't suitable. The dark-skinned woman got up, shook out her clothes, and went on her way. Time was passing, and he had to leave too. He looked at his watch. His flight was at six. If he missed it, he'd miss the party at Darwish's. He had to be at the air-port two hours before to get through security. It would be best to go now, before rush hour. The woman was heading in his direction. He peered up at her to find she was looking at him. He nodded at her politely, and she reacted with an astonished frown. Then she stopped and looked at him again.

"Can it really be you?"

"Me?"

"Yes. McCain Boy."

"I think you've got the wrong person. My name's not McCain."

"Right. You're 'Fool,' but me and my friends called you 'McCain Boy.'"

"Wait . . . you're . . ."

"Yep, 'red girl.' That's me, Fool."

She burst out laughing as she said it, then spontaneously hugged him. He was embarrassed and returned her hug cautiously.

She told him her whole story. She'd lived in the neighborhood while she was a kid, then had to gone to school New York. She'd settled down there, gotten married, and had kids. Then, when the marriage went bad, she moved back to DC, to the home she'd grown up in, and found a federal government job. She still lived here with her two kids. No, she wasn't an Indian—either from India or a Native American tribe. She was from Oklahoma, in fact.

"That day the school made us bring in a dish that represented our family heritage and, man, you brought in a McCain readymade cake. That was some joke. Me and my friends laughed about it all night. What was that all about?"

"Sad to say it wasn't a joke. In fact, my mom made something called mulukhiya, but my dad lost his temper for some reason, and threw the dish at her. So then I had nothing to bring. I bought a cake from a little grocery store on the way. I was the only one who ate any of it."

"I don't know which is worse: your mom's dish getting tossed or you buying that crappy cake. But it made you famous, and most of my friends thought you were doing it to mess with the teachers. Some kind of send-up. I mean, they treat us like foreigners, and think we come from places where they have all kinds of strange foods. So they set up some kind of party to celebrate our 'traditions,' you know, and all that. We thought you bringing a McCain cake, the most down-home, ordinary cake in America, was so smartass. Real clever."

"Really?"

"Man, you can't imagine. McCain Boy. Son of McCain. Some timid handsome little brown kid messing with the school's racial stereotyping in such a clever way. Made a hero out of you. You could have asked any one of us out back then—it would have been quite an honor!"

She carried on talking about the school and how dumb kids were at that age. Her son was going to the same school and she was pleased about that.

"The school has been tough on them, but really school is tough for everyone. Kids can be very cruel to one another. What can you do?"

She said she was really glad to talk to him and asked what he was doing there. She suggested they go for a coffee and said she knew a place within walking distance. But he had a plane to catch, what a shame.

She told him her friend Patty wouldn't believe it when she told her she'd come across him again.

"You don't remember Patty? The skinny blond girl I always hung out with? She had such a crush on you for the whole last two years of school. Well, she'll remember you, all right. You had so many good things going for you."

Then she asked: "Where do you live now?"

"Detroit."

"You could not have chosen a place any farther away. Are there lots of Arabs there, like they say? Man, it's really good to speak to you after all these years. Shame we can't grab a coffee, talk about old times a little. McCain Boy. What a coincidence!"

They shook hands and she hurried off down the hill. He put his raincoat on, put his hands in his pockets, and went off to catch his plane.

7

Rabab al-Omri

RABAB ARRIVED AT THE AIRPORT at exactly five o'clock, one hour before the plane took off for New York. She was cutting it fine, as the new airport security procedures alone might take forty-five minutes. Rabab didn't care, however: she was adamant that an hour before takeoff was enough. If the airport authorities wanted to make things more complicated, that was their problem. If she missed the plane because of them, she'd sue them.

Rabab hated airports, and airplanes. She normally went to New York by train, but she was going to LA afterward, and her office said the train to New York was too expensive, so she gave in to the office cost cutters. Another plane journey wouldn't kill her. She'd get in at six fifty, so she could be at her old professor Darwish's place by seven thirty. She'd have dinner and see Salma, Darwish's niece and the daughter of Leila, her close friend since college days. The next day she had two meetings, then was off to LA for two full days of meetings, then back to DC.

Travel exhausted her, but there was no way around it. It set her teeth on edge: getting to the airport, the ridiculous security procedures, the long walkways, looking for the gate, being crammed into a crowded plane, wedged into a narrow seat next to an often rude fellow traveler, tasteless airplane food, and the disruption of her daily routine. And then landing, waiting for the doors to open, finding the luggage belt, waiting for the bags, then dragging them around, looking for an exit sign among all the other signs and boards; finding a taxi and explaining where the address was; getting into the hotel, showing her ID and filling out the register, giving her credit card number, looking for her room, dealing with the bellboy waiting for a tip, unpacking clothes and makeup and papers. She didn't like hotels: sleeping in a strange bed in a room that was almost always too hot or too cold, and where the AC always seemed to blow right at you. She'd lie there every time, asking herself if hotel designers were all stupid. And then there was the hotel food, which always managed to combine being unjustifiably expensive, humdrum, and unvarying.

Next came the meetings themselves, usually with strangers who would judge everything about you: how well turned out you were, the way you talked, your accent, the color of your skin, how clever your remarks were, how warm you were as a person, how liberated and go-getting you came across. While they weighed her up, she'd get down to business: to try to convince them that Arab-American rights needed to be protected. They'd nod—they'd always nod—while not being at all convinced. After she'd made her pitch, they'd make amenable, or seemingly amenable, noises, before citing something or other that prevented them from doing what she asked: company regulations, state regulations, university regulations, competition considerations, lack of time. This. That. Anything. She'd keep going at it until it became clear they weren't going to offer anything, and so she'd move into phase two: the threat of a lawsuit. The tone would change at that point. Some would become more flexible, others more obdurate. After that came phase three: direct threats. Then the tone would change yet again. Occasionally—rarely—it would end in agreement. Most of the time it would end with her being ejected from the building, triggering a lawsuit from her office.

She got to the airport, pushed her cart with her suitcase on it to the self-check-in machine, thus cutting the number of staff she had to deal with. She chose her seat, swiped her credit card, got her boarding pass, and headed for departures. She stood in the security line. Luckily it was short and moving pretty quickly. A man about her age stood in the line behind her. Tall, dark complexion; he looked like an Arab. He was strangely attractive and wore a raincoat. He looked at her and nodded politely without saying anything. She returned the gesture and turned back again to the line ahead. It seemed strange to her that a guy would wear a raincoat on a hot, rainless Washington day. The line was moving fast. She took her shoes off, put them and her handbag through the scanner, and took her laptop out of her hand luggage and put that through as well. She looked at the security women, who nodded to her, then walked through the scanner. No alarm sounded. Rabab went over to collect her things from the scanner belt while observing at the Arab-looking man. He seemed confused by the many things he had to do all at the same time, delaying the line and irritating the security staff. He walked through the scanner and it emitted a piercing alarm. He remembered something he had in his pocket and removed it, went back through the scanner, and set the alarm off again, delaying the people waiting even more. A security agent stopped him, saying in a loud, robot-like voice, "Sir. Please step aside. Stand there, please. Yes, right there. Yes, to the side. No, leave your things there, and we'll deal with them."

Rabab turned around, her bags in her hand, and asked, "What's that about? Why are you pulling him aside?"

"Ma'am, if you've been through security, please don't hang around here. Please move ahead."

"Yes, I've finished, but I'm asking you why you've pulled that guy aside."

"Ma'am, this is a security procedure."

"Is this because he looks Arab?"

"Ma'am, please. There's no need for that kind of talk."

"I am asking you a question."

"Is he with you? Do you know this gentleman? Please step aside too, take your things, and come this way."

"Why? I've been through security. Do you doubt your own security procedures?"

"Ma'am, can I see your passport and boarding pass, please?"

The Arab-looking man intervened for the first time at that point: "Ma'am, please don't bother."

"Can you both step aside, please?" said the security guard.

So, between her comments, his bid to keep her out of it, and the security agent's edginess, the two of them ended up in a small room guarded by two security agents: one male, one female.

Rabab offered her hand to the man she'd gotten herself caught up with. "Rabab al-Omri, lawyer."

The man was on the point of shaking her outstretched hand when a security agent told them to be quiet, so he hesitated, then put his hand back down to his side. Rabab held her open hand out in the air for a second before noticing her new companion had turned his attention toward the agent, and so she withdrew it. The man hesitated again for a moment, but then timidly held out his hand. "Adnan Fikri, accountant."

She asked him where he was going, and he replied tersely: "New York." She said she was going there too, and asked him if he was from DC: a polite way of asking which country he was from originally. He replied that he was born and raised in DC, but that he'd moved away many years ago. She nodded and said few people born in DC stayed there for life. She waited for him to say which country he was from originally, or to ask her the same thing, but he kept quiet. He didn't look at her, or at anything else in particular. He occasionally looked at the door of the room near the security scanner that the two of them had been shepherded to. At other times he looked straight ahead blankly. He was confused, unsure whether to be grateful for her attempt to help him, or resentful for her making the problem worse by her unsolicited intervention. Rabab tried to lighten the mood, but he didn't reply. After a few minutes, a security agent came in and took him aside. He asked Adnan a few questions, then directed him to where his baggage was. Adnan left without looking at her. She shook her head archly and carried on waiting. Another security man came up shortly afterward, and pointed at Rabab with contempt he didn't bother concealing. He gave her back her papers and told her to be on her way. She asked what had happened to Adnan, and he muttered something inaudible and hurried back to his security gate.

She walked around the airport walkways looking for the departure gate. Where had Adnan gone? And what kind of name was that? Palestinian? He seemed about the same age as her, maybe a year or two older. There was something odd about the way he way was dressed but she couldn't put her finger on exactly what was wrong with his clothes. His clothes and bearing suggested he wasn't married, or at any rate didn't have a woman to take care of him. Maybe he had a wife with no sense of style. Or maybe his wife had followed him from the old country and didn't know what people wore here. Maybe it was his stature, the way he carried himself. But there was something attractive about him, though she couldn't figure out what. She found him staring at the departure screens, and quickly headed straight over to him. She spotted the New York departure gate number before he did. "Fifty-five. Over there," she said, pointing toward the gate. He noticed her, and smiled hesitantly.

They walked over to the gate. Only twenty minutes to take-off. They would reach the plane and split up, perhaps for good. Curiosity overtook her. She asked if he lived in New York, and he just said no. Silence. She didn't give in, though, and asked why he was going to New York. Slowly, slowly, like pulling teeth, she found out they were both going to Professor Darwish's dinner party. He explained that Darwish was his mother's uncle, and learned from her that she was both an old student of Darwish's and a friend of Leila's. She was going to Salma's birthday party too, and was amazed at the coincidence that had brought them together at the airport. She imagined that the conversation would become easier from then onward, but in fact he shut up altogether, right up to the departure gate.

The gate was crowded, with children screaming and running around everywhere. A few people were sitting on the ground because there were no seats free. They both went up to the desk clerk and asked at the same time when the plane would leave. They found out that it would be forty-five minutes late and exchanged annoyed remarks. It meant they'd both be late for the dinner party, but the clerk just shrugged and said there was nothing she could do. Rabab looked at Adnan and told him she had access to the business-class lounge and could sign him in as a guest. She made a gallant "be my guest" type of gesture, but Adnan seemed unsure, and wasn't convinced he could get into the business lounge when he was traveling coach. She assured him it was within the rules, and that she wasn't going to smuggle him in, yet he still seemed very reluctant. She told him that she didn't want to impose: if he'd really rather spend forty-five minutes among screaming brats instead of having a drink while reading the paper or checking his emails in a comfortable lounge, she wouldn't deprive him of the pleasure. He mumbled something about not wanting a service he wasn't entitled to. She looked at him exasperatedly as he walked along with her.

In the lounge, she asked what he wanted to drink; he thanked her and said he'd just read the paper. She got herself a white wine and some water. He fetched a paper and sat next to her, but she started talking before he got the chance to read anything. She said that, unlike him, she'd been born in Egypt, but had come over to Washington and settled there. She couldn't put up with Egypt anymore. He nodded and said "yes" repeatedly, though she hadn't said anything that needed his agreement. She looked at him, wondering what he was thinking. Did he think she was being pushy, or was he just shy, odd? After a short exchange in Arabic, they went back to speaking English. He said a few words about his work as an accountant for a big Detroit car company, and even fewer about his family and old life in DC. They talked about Washington at some length, especially Dupont Circle, where she lived and which he seemed particularly to love. She wondered if he had a special memory of that neighborhood. Maybe a first love. It suddenly occurred to her that he looked like her ex, Alex. That annoyed her, and it showed. Adnan thought he must have said something to irritate her, so he went quiet. After a few seconds of awkward silence, he began reading his paper and she took her phone out and started checking her email.

But then she started up again: "Have you lived in Detroit a long time?"

"Yes. About twenty-five years."

"Oh my God! Twenty-five years in the same place? Aren't you bored of it?"

"Boredom can be found everywhere."

Not a bad reply, she thought, but then he went quiet again, and she started to feel like she was being a nuisance, so she shut up too. After five minutes, he took the initiative and asked her about her job. She said she worked for a legal firm that defended minority rights, and that she specialized in defending Arab and Muslim Americans. He seemed somewhat interested in that, so she carried on talking about her work, how hard it was, and how much harder it had become since 9/11. He nodded several times, and commented that minorities in general always faced difficulties. She asked him what he meant, and he said minorities were doomed to face discrimination. She became angry at this, and asked him, switching back to Egyptian Arabic, "What are you saying? You think it's OK that they trample all over us? Should we also apologize for inconveniencing them? Tell them: 'Please, step all over us'?"

"I didn't mean that. But discrimination is everywhere, from the grocery store to the security forces, and not everything can be solved with a lawsuit."

"It's nonsense like that that holds us back."

"Why are you being aggressive?"

"I'm not being aggressive. I just have no patience with this kind of talk. I was done with these debates at the age of twenty-five."

She looked at him and sensed him retreating back into himself, as if his very features were shrinking. He slipped into complete silence. After a minute, he said he'd go and check if the flight was due to take off. She told him that there was no point in asking, as it wouldn't leave for another quarter of an hour. He said that he wanted to buy something anyway, and hesitantly got up, nodding in her direction. She nodded back, and he hurried off. She went back to her emails, audibly grumbling, "What an idiot!"

She asked herself what was up with men. Alex was just like this awkward guy: attractive, kindhearted, well-intentioned, and smart, but lacking something. She had told herself back then that it didn't matter. Alex knew her well, was understanding, and looked after her. He involved himself in her life, and didn't come with any of the issues or complications you normally got with Middle Eastern men. They'd been friends at first. He'd put up with all her flaws and problems, and then, like in a B movie, their friendship turned to love. She thought he was the one. They got married quickly, despite Leila's objections. She hadn't even been sure herself she'd made the right choice, but she rushed into the wedding before Leila could convince her otherwise.

It didn't last much more than a year and a few months. Four months after they got married, she lost her job at the prestigious law firm she'd worked for since graduating. She had been dedicated and hardworking, but her boss told her one morning that they had to make cutbacks in the number of lawyers and that her job was going. Two months later she met up with an old university classmate, who told her she'd been appointed to the same firm, doing what was practically her old job. She was shocked, couldn't understand, and at first was riddled with doubt that she had the right skills. Her efforts to find another job similar to the one she'd lost came to nothing. Alex backed her all the way, but her sense of failure grew until she stopped looking altogether, and ended up spending all her time at home. She looked back on that as the lowest point in her life. On top of that, Leila went back to live in Egypt around that time, saying she had no reason to stay in America anymore, and that she would return to the one place where she could make a difference. That hurt Rabab too, as she felt Leila must see their friendship as unimportant, but also because Leila had decided on this unilaterally without talking to her friend, underlining her own sense of worthlessness. She was adrift in her life, with nothing to occupy her.

Then one evening she met up with Christie. It wasn't until Christie was drunk that she confessed to Rabab that the office had gotten rid of her because of her "foreign" origins. She said a number of clients had appeared reluctant to give her cases, either because they lacked confidence in her abilities or because they didn't think they could connect with her to the same degree as those who spoke and acted the same way as them. After a while she became a financial and administrative burden to the firm, but they couldn't justify getting rid of her. So they got rid of the post itself, only to reinstate it two months later. Christie confessed she felt bad for Rabab, but she knew what things were like at the office. Rabab was also drunk when Christie told her all of this, but she felt like she had just woken up from a long sleep. When Christie finished speaking, Rabab stood up, got her things together, and started to leave. Christie asked her to give her a lift, since she was in no state to drive, or even get a taxi. And at that point Rabab exploded into a sudden torrent of abuse, which shocked everyone in the bar, herself included. Everyone around them fell silent while Rabab rained down insults on Christie for her lack of understanding, before picking up her purse and leaving.

Rabab relayed the whole story that same night to Alex, who patiently but skeptically heard her out. Rabab couldn't exactly understand Alex's response, but he continued to doubt the truth of her story, while at the same time appearing to realize that there was a link between her ethnicity and her inability to find a job that matched her qualifications. Worse than that, at least in Rabab's eyes, he seemed to have accepted this. He had even begun discouraging her from applying for prestigious positions on the grounds that she was "wasting her time," because "of course they won't accept you at that firm."

Day by day, Rabab's anger grew. Leila had left, but Rabab resolved she would not do the same. She wouldn't give in. She wouldn't accept what Alex the coward had accepted. She confronted him about it more than once, and they argued often. He accused her of suffering from a persecution complex, and she accused him of not being man enough. Things continued to slide, and they got divorced, right around the same time Leila wrote to her to tell her she'd agreed to marry Luqman.

Rabab often thought her and Leila's lives kind of complemented each other, as if they'd had to divide their lot between them. While Leila, pregnant with Salma, had quit her job in Egypt, Rabab had set aside her personal life altogether and carved out a life defending the rights of minorities. If she'd gotten pregnant by Alex, her kid would be about Salma's age. Rabab didn't marry again, though she did have a relationship that nearly went that way, around the time Leila and Luqman split up. Ever since, Rabab had lived on her own. She didn't want anyone running her life or holding her to account. Inside, though, she often asked herself if she had gone down the wrong road in life.

"Where has that idiot Adnan gone?" she asked herself, looking at her watch. It was time to board. She got up and walked toward the desk clerk and asked her innocently if she knew when the New York flight would finally take off. Confused, the clerk looked at her and said, "New York?" Rabab stared at her like she was stupid, and mutely nodded. The clerk looked at her computer screen and asked Rabab for her boarding pass. When Rabab gave it to her, the clerk looked at it carefully, then at her computer again. She called over an older colleague and showed her both the boarding pass and the computer screen. The older member of staff looked at Rabab, half in amazement and half in contempt. "Madam, the New York flight left a quarter hour ago."

"What?"

"We put out a passenger call more than once."

"But the girl at the gate said it wouldn't leave until six forty-five at the earliest."

"Yes, but the plane got an earlier slot. We put out a call to passengers, and then the plane took off. Everyone else boarded."

"Well, I didn't because your colleague told me six forty-five. It's now six forty."

"I'm afraid the plane's left."

"OK. What are you going to do about it?"

"There are no more planes to New York tonight. The first is at nine in the morning."

"Tomorrow? I have commitments in New York tonight."

"Ma'am, there's no plane to New York from this airport tonight."

"What the hell are you saying?"

"I'm sorry, but there's nothing I can do for you."

She left, leaving Rabab astonished, standing and staring at the embarrassed desk clerk while her older colleague went back to her computer. Was this a joke? A wave of anger washed over her, but she kept control of herself.

"Please, ma'am."

"What am I supposed to do now?"

"I don't know. I guess you'll have to spend the night in DC and come back in the morning."

"And what about my commitment in New York?"

"I don't know. Maybe there's another flight from Dulles."

"Can you arrange that for me?"

"Sorry, ma'am. That's not our responsibility."

"Even when you give your passengers the wrong information?"

"Ma'am, we put out a passenger call more than once, and you didn't respond. Where were you?"

"Where was I? Am I meant to sit here by the desk listening for passenger calls, which are impossible to hear anyway? Even when you told me the flight would take off in forty-five minutes?"

"Everyone else came."

"Really? What if I had been deaf? What if I was hard of hearing? What's your policy for the hearing impaired? Shouldn't the hearing impaired be allowed to catch your planes when their slot is put back then brought forward again?"

"There's nothing I can do to help you, ma'am."

"You can tell me how I lodge a complaint about this."

"You can find the details on our website. Now, please excuse me, I have other work to."

And she left. Rabab felt like her head would explode. They can't do this kind of thing. They can't just toss her out on the street like this. Shouldn't they at least say sorry and accept responsibility?

Rabab left the lounge and went to the customer-service center. She stood waiting in a line, fuming. It took a full quarter of an hour to get to the desk. The desk clerk was a bit more sympathetic, but did not disagree with his colleague's approach. He said company policy and the terms and conditions of the ticket absolved the airline from responsibility in a case like this. Because the fault lay with the passenger. He went back over the passenger call and Rabab's failure to respond to it. Well, damn them all: Rabab would write a letter of complaint later. If she could have gotten away with it, she'd have given that desk clerk a bloody nose. Instead, she walked off and went back to the lounge.

She checked online for any other flight out of Dulles, or anything that would get her to New York before eight. Then suddenly she remembered Adnan. He must have caught the plane, as he'd been so determined to hang around the departure gate. He must have heard the call. Of course, he didn't for a minute think about coming to find her. There were no flights that would get her in at a reasonable hour, but she might be able to catch the seven thirty train. She'd keep all the tickets and receipts and send them to the airline. If they wouldn't pay up, she'd sue them.

She carried her hand luggage over to the exit. On the way, she glanced at the older supervisor she had first complained to, whose face, she was sure, had something of a gloating expression.

She felt so angry at this woman. How can a member of staff treat one of her passengers like that? What had she done to her? She could sue her, but she knew it was a waste of time. She couldn't prove bad faith or oppressive treatment in court, even in a formal complaint to the airline. You can't prove that someone is treating you hatefully; you just have to suffer their hatred in silence. And she had suffered it, just like she'd suffered the supercilious glance of victory from that hateful woman. She remembered Adnan and what he'd said about discrimination. How you could never end it. That made her even angrier. With that stupid woman, with Adnan, and with herself. She consoled herself by resolving never to fly with that airline again. Then she left departures.

So what was she going to do now? She didn't have her clothes with her because the damn airline had put her bag on the plane. She couldn't buy anything, now or in the morning: no time. She would have wear these clothes all evening and all day tomorrow, when she had important meetings to go to. She couldn't walk into a meeting room dressed like this, not after the evening she was going to have. She'd have to buy clothes somewhere in New York in the morning, first thing. The whole thing was so annoying.

She decided to go straight to the train station. On her way out to the taxi rank, she noticed Adnan sitting at one end of the hall. How come he hadn't caught the plane either? She thought about leaving him there, but changed her mind and came back. She went over to him and asked him in Arabic, "So you missed it too?"

He looked at her and made a hand gesture that said yes. She asked what he was going to do. He said he'd changed his ticket to go straight back to Detroit. But what about the dinner party? He'd contact Professor Darwish to apologize. He didn't want to get the train with her, because it didn't get in until midnight. The party would be over. He had to go to Detroit the next day, so there was no point in going at all. She stood in front of him for a moment, not knowing what to say. She didn't even know what she wanted from him. "Enough, just go," she said to herself. She said good-bye to him for the last time, wished him luck, and headed off to the taxi rank.

There was just one taxi, and the driver was half asleep. She got in and asked for Union Station. They reached the train station in a half hour. When the train left with Rabab onboard, she finally felt like she was back in control of things a little. She wouldn't get to New York before midnight, of course, and she'd miss out on Darwish's party and seeing Salma. She wouldn't even have time to see her the day after, as she had to catch the LA flight, and Salma would be gone by the time she got back. She thought about calling and apologizing, but she couldn't find the courage within herself to face the legendary wrath of Professor Darwish. She'd call tomorrow and explain. She'd get to Penn Station at midnight. It would be deserted at that time. She'd take a taxi—probably the only one there—and go to her hotel. She'd be exhausted by then. It was going to be an exhausting night. She closed her eyes to stop herself thinking about it all. She fell asleep.

8

Midnight at Penn Station

AT MIDNIGHT—THAT IS, IN exactly half an hour—Salma was going to turn twenty-one. She looked at her watch again; it was her own fault she was late. Grandpa must be really mad. If she hadn't gotten the platform wrong, she wouldn't have missed the three-thirty train, and would have gotten to New York on time. She would have made it to her own birthday party, which her grandfather had spent two weeks preparing. He had invited a lot of people: almost anyone she had any kind of relationship with in America. He hated it when people weren't punctual, let alone four hours late. She'd get in at midnight, the guests would be gone, and Grandpa would perhaps be in bed already. Thank God he'd given her a key; she wouldn't dare wake him up at that late hour. Maybe she shouldn't blame herself; she had gotten confused by all the platforms and signs. And they don't let passengers onto the platform until ten minutes before the train's due to leave, so everyone crowds around the gates. And if you make a mistake, like she had, it was difficult to get to the right place on time. And there's no one you can ask. When she realized she was on the wrong track, she ran over to the right one, but the train doors were already locked for departure. She stood in front of the door, knocking; the conductor was standing inside looking at her, smiling and shaking his head. The train set off and left her standing on the platform. Just like that.

She went back to the station concourse, teary-eyed. Luckily, Jessie was still sitting in the coffee shop and Salma explained what had happened. Jessie comforted her and cursed Mr. Train Company Boss Man, while Salma laughed through her tears. Jessie bought her a new ticket on the next train, insisting it was her fault Salma was late, and refused to take money for the new ticket.

The real problem was that the next train left Washington at seven thirty, arriving in New York close to midnight. Salma panicked. "Grandpa will kill me!"

Jessie reassured her that he would do no such thing—not because she was late at least. She called him to explain on Salma's behalf. He was not happy. Jessie could tell from his terseness that he was angry but trying to suppress his annoyance. He asked Jessie why Salma had waited until the last minute to travel: why hadn't she caught a morning train? How exactly had she managed to miss the train, when everyone else had managed to catch it? What guarantee was there that she'd catch the next train, as she seemed to have a problem making it to the right platform? Jessie used all her charms on Salma's grumpy grandfather until he backed down a little. But he did ask Jessie to tell Salma that the birthday party was ruined because of her, that he'd have to let the guests know, and that she should try not to mess anything else up before she arrived.

"My God, your grandpa is tough."

"Oh, that's nothing."

Jessie—Yasmine, originally—was Lebanese-American, a friend of Salma's father. She was warmhearted, open, and welcoming. She looked much younger than her forty-five years. Jessie took Salma on a tour of DC the first day they met, driving her around the capital's sights. Her grandfather had never taken her anywhere in New York. He'd given her a map and a subway pass, and left her to tour the city by herself. The one place he did take her was the Museum of Modern Art, where she saw a photo exhibition that made no sense to her at all. Other than that, he left her to herself. In the evenings he'd ask a few curt questions: How was her day? Was she hungry? Then he'd leave her to it and go to bed. Her dad rarely saw her, because her mother insisted that she not stay with him, and he was usually busy at the hospital during the day.

Jessie took her to Dupont Circle the day they met. They lunched in a restaurant that also sold secondhand books, and Jessie told Salma her American story, starting with her grandfather, who had immigrated in the early 1900s with fifteen dollars in his pocket. A highly respected doctor in his little Lebanese village, he left it all behind, fleeing the chains of Ottoman rule in search of a better life. Jessie told her how, despite all that, he had gone back to find a girl in his old village when he had wanted to get married. Jessie's father had done the same.

"They're all like that, young Arab men," Jessie said. "They want a girlfriend from over here, but when it comes to marriage they want a girl from the farm back home. Poor misguided fools, all of them."

Salma asked her what she meant, but Jessie had just laughed. She said she didn't want to corrupt her. Salma then asked her whether she felt Lebanese or American. Did she want to go back to Lebanon one day? Jessie laughed again and said, "Lebanon? My God, no! I wake up every morning thanking God I don't live in an Arab country!"

Salma told Jessie about Mahmoud, her classmate at business school, with whom she was in love; she told her about the problems she had with him, about her own problems, and the problems with her girlfriends and her mom and dad. "The contradictions of life for Egyptian girls," as she put it. Sometimes she felt "close to God," and wanted to become closer to Him, and to stop doing things that would anger Him. Other times, she felt such things were nothing but restrictive. When Jessie asked what kind of things she meant, Salma answered, "Everything. All the rules. I sometimes feel like my life is run by an unending series of rules and restrictions, and that I'm the only one living like this."

She went on that people broke the rules all the time, but her mother thought they all abided by them. Salma knew differently. She saw how it was for her girlfriends. She knew how free they were to do all kind of things, in secret of course. At the same time, Salma didn't want that for herself. She didn't want to deceive her mother or betray her father's trust, but she didn't want to live her life in chains either. She didn't know what to do. Salma fell silent, then added, as if revealing a secret, that she knew a girl in Brooklyn—one of Aunt Amira's inner circle—who had told her a week ago that she envied her turning twenty-one. Salma asked her why, and she replied that she was waiting impatiently to be that age so that she could run away from the family home. Salma was horrified, and asked her why. She answered that she didn't want to be a Muslim. "Can you imagine it? I asked her why, and she said she didn't want to follow a religion that made her feel guilty all the time." Salma fell silent again, and Jessie patted her shoulder, silent too.

Jessie asked Salma about her father and whether she had talked to him about all of this, but Salma told her that she felt like he was never there. Sure, he was living in New York, but she hardly ever managed to see him. Jessie asked, cautiously, how her mother was, and whether she was as strict as was rumored. Salma laughed and said her mother was more temperamental than strict.

Salma had talked and asked questions as they toured the city: the White House, Congress, the Supreme Court, the Lincoln Memorial, the Jefferson Memorial, Arlington National Cemetery—where the dead of the many American wars lie—the World Bank, and the Holocaust Memorial Museum. It made Salma so happy to see, for the first time, so many of the places she'd been hearing about all her life. She showered Jessie with questions, and Jessie would laugh and take her on to the next new place and treat her to food, all the while answering her questions.

Then it was the day of Salma's journey back to New York, her taciturn grandfather, her absent father, and her subway map. How had the time passed so quickly? She tried to negotiate a longer stay over the phone with her grandfather, but he ruled it out flatly. She knew it was difficult; she had other commitments in New York—there was her father and her aunt Amira, her grandmother's sister. When Salma missed the train, Jessie took her for another treat: kayaking on the Potomac. Salma's heart soared, and she yelled with joy as they set off together in the narrow little boat. Salma hadn't the first idea about rowing, but she followed Jessie's lead.

After a while they stopped midstream for a break and a look around. Salma thought the river was beautiful, and Jessie nodded when she told her so. Salma got up the courage to broach a subject she hadn't dared to bring up before, something that took Jessie by surprise. She cautiously said she'd heard her mother talking to her father on the telephone before she set off on this trip, railing against him for letting Salma stay with Jessie while she was in DC. Her original plan for Salma to stay with her old friend Rabab had unraveled when Rabab had to go out of town at the last moment. Salma's mother had asked him angrily how he could let Salma stay with "a woman like her." Salma asked what her mother meant; Jessie stayed silent for a while, then calmly said that people wanted different things, and that everyone should know and seek what they wanted, not what others wanted for them. Some people, like her mother, did not accept that people wanted different things. Then she cheerfully asked Salma to start rowing, otherwise the boat would turn around on itself. They didn't return to the topic again.

Salma felt her whole trip had been full of contradictions. Her grandfather had suggested it, and her mother had strongly opposed it, yet had backed down under his intense pressure. Salma found her mother's relationship with Grandpa Darwish strange, and would quiz her mother about it, without ever getting a clear answer. When she asked her mom why she never went to New York, Leila replied that she didn't like the city. But how could she not like it when she had lived there herself for ten years? In the end, her mother agreed that she could go, though only under the joint supervision of Salma's grandfather and her aunt Amira and her husband, who were utterly different from her grandfather. At the same time, despite the fact that Salma's father was in New York, her mother wouldn't let her stay with him. And she got her way on that. Salma could see him, and go out in the day with him, but wasn't to stay with him. She didn't understand why everyone gave in to her mother like that—even her father, and even after they were divorced. She had promised herself to ask him, but never dared to. She thought about asking Jessie, but didn't dare do that either. She thought about asking Aunt Amira, but she was conservative, with deeply held traditional values, which wouldn't have allowed her to answer such questions.

When the time for the train finally came, Jessie stopped the car in front of Union Station, waking Salma up from her thoughts. They went into the station and sat in the main café until the train was due. Jessie hugged her and walked with her as far as she could, then waved her off onto the platform. Salma loved Jessie, but felt afraid. She would love to become strong and independent like Jessie when she got older, but she didn't want to be seen as "improper," to use her mother's phrase. She wanted to be special in a way that was lovable, not to have people whispering about her behind her back. She wanted to have kids, not end up single like Jessie. Nonetheless, she had loved their three days together, which had passed like a dream, and from which she was slowly waking up to find herself in an almost-empty train car.

The time approached midnight, as she approached twenty-one years of age. She'd get to Penn Station at eleven twenty-five. She called her grandfather twice on the way. He talked to her the first time, but didn't answer the second call. Maybe he was busy with his guests. She was sorry now that she had missed her party. Poor Grandpa. He'd gone to all this trouble for her, and she'd ruined it. She contacted her aunt Amira, who warned her about Penn Station at that time of night. The station empties of passengers and staff, and attracts junkies and drunks. Even taxis didn't hang around at that time because there were very few people arriving. Amira suggested she go straight from the platform to the main exit, because the other exits would be locked before midnight. If she did that, everything would be all right, Salma told herself. Yet she still blamed herself. How could she have made such a dumb mistake?

When Salma stayed with Aunt Amira in Brooklyn, she had taken her to the mosque where her husband, Sheikh Daoud, was the imam. She introduced her to a few of the Arab girls there who were studying in America. On the way home, Aunt Amira asked whether she liked America. When she replied that she did, Amira said she thought America was a beautiful country filled with blessings that its people didn't appreciate. Amira asked her about her university in Egypt and, after listening carefully to Salma's reply, responded that it was a shame she hadn't studied in America, where the opportunities to learn were endless. She told her about Egyptians who lived and studied in America and then did amazing things for their families, their home country, and their wider community. Sheikh Daoud broke into the conversation at that point: "Some people think that because America is not a Muslim country it's no place for Muslims. It's quite the opposite: this is God's land and he gave it to His followers. The Muslims have to build and create in America like any other people who come here. Look around you and you'll see every nationality here, thanks be to God. People from every corner of the world are here building, innovating, creating. Muslims shouldn't cut themselves off from all that."

Amira then asked her flat out whether she had thought about staying and finishing her studies in America, and whether she thought her mother would agree to it. Amira knew her mother's reservations about life in America—after all, she herself had gone back to live in Egypt. Salma fell silent, wondering why her aunt had changed her mind about her coming to America. Amira was against Salma coming to begin with, and now she wanted her to live here. Amira asked her again, and Salma said she had thought about it, and then went quiet. They talked in the car, on their way to a hike. This was during the weekend Salma spent with them in Brooklyn, as stipulated by her mother. Everything was complicated with her mother. Every single thing she wanted to do had to be negotiated and debated. The car crossed Brooklyn Bridge; a light rain spattered the windshield and the voice of a preacher on the radio extolled the virtues of jihad. Daoud seemed tense as he drove, craning toward the windshield to be able to see.

"Shall I get your glasses for you?" Amira asked.

"Yes, God bless you. We don't want the girl to think I'm a bad driver."

He smiled, as did Amira. He turned the wipers on and they made a repetitive sound as they swept back and forth across the glass. The preacher's voice continued, and Amira put her arm around Salma's shoulders. Salma felt a little suffocated.

"I don't think Mom would agree, or Dad. And it would be really expensive."

"What grade did you get this year?"

Salma replied that she had gotten an "excellent" again this year, and Amira congratulated her, patting her shoulder and saying that Salma could maybe get a scholarship in America for her master's, if she wanted. There were charities that offered that kind of thing and Daoud knew some of the people running them. If she kept her grades up, he could maybe help her get one. She would have to be more "committed religiously," but in return the charity would pay all her expenses through to graduation. They'd help her find a job too, and to settle down in America. "And I've got a husband in mind for you. He's good looking and one of our people. He was born here, and he's a committed Muslim: you'd get citizenship. When you're a little older. We could think about you getting engaged in your last year of college, and then you could get married after graduation." Amira gave her a sidelong wink as she said all this.

Salma thanked her briskly, but Amira insisted she give it some proper thought, adding that she would broach the subject with her mother.

The train stopped again, and Salma could make out a large sign through the window: Penn Station, short for Pennsylvania. Dragging her suitcase behind her, she quickly got off the train, and walked assuredly down the platform toward the exit sign. The train moved out and she felt a gust of wind buffet her a little. She smiled to herself confidently, thinking: "I am in America, in a train station. I've traveled from Washington to New York on my own. I sorted everything out myself: luggage, tickets, money. I've followed a map and met people I've never met before. I've traveled from one country to another, from airport to airport, from one station to another. I'm crossing streets I've never seen before. I talk to Americans in their own language. Where's that scared little girl holding on to Mommy's hand now?"

She smiled, pleased with herself, and felt a sense of power surge through her. She took her iPod out of her bag, and put the little white plugs in her ears. She started listening to Wust El Balad; she loved that band. The station signs seemed a little different from the day she'd left for DC. She stopped to check she was going the right way, buttoned up her gray raincoat, and headed for the main door. The cold hit her as she exited. There was a taxi waiting on the stand, so she headed straight for it, opened the door, nodded a greeting to the driver, just like Jessie had told her to do, and got in.

"Corner of Riverside and Seventy-Ninth, please."

"Huh?"

"Riverside and Seventy-Ninth."

"Where's that?"

"Where is it? Manhattan! West Side."

"Manhattan? Lady, we're in New Jersey!"

"New Jersey? What? Isn't this Penn Station?"

"Yeah: Penn Station, New Jersey. You should have gotten off at the station after: Penn Station, New York."

"Really? Why are there two stations with the same name? OK, please take me and I'll pay you."

"That'll cost you serious money. Plus, I don't have time to go there and back, and I won't find anyone to ride back with me. You're better off getting back on the train. It's only one stop."

She got out of the taxi, exasperated, her feelings of bravery evaporated. She blamed herself again: "How could I be so stupid?" The unfamiliar train station now seemed completely deserted. She went to the one ticket window still lit up and asked the woman behind it about the next train to Penn Station, New York. She replied that the train was due in less than ten minutes, and that she had better run because it was the last train and the station would close afterward. Salma quickly bought a ticket and asked her which platform it was. The clerk pointed to the opposite corner of the station concourse. It seemed really dark over there, so she asked again which platform it was exactly, but couldn't make out what the clerk muttered from behind the glass. She asked again, but the woman wasn't listening and had begun packing up her things. Salma headed off to where the clerk had pointed. The fast-food places were all closed, leaving little light. Everyone had left. A newspaper stand, a pharmacy, and a few other shops—it was hard to make out what they sold—had all closed. The station seemed bleak, like a movie set: the stage for a murder or rape scene.

Salma reached the corner and saw a sign to the platform, but she wasn't sure it was the right one. She looked at the ticket, but it had numbers plastered all over it, and she couldn't distinguish the platform number from the one for the train, or the sales clerk, or the ticket itself. She went down a walkway that led to some steps descending into complete darkness. Her heart trembled a little as she went down the first step, praying it was the right way. There were only a few minutes left and, if she missed the train, how would she get to her grandfather's? And where would she spend the night? Halfway down the stairs, she heard loud voices behind her. Without thinking, she turned and saw four young men shouting and pushing each other around at the top of the stairs: huge guys in football shirts with large numbers on them, and pants hanging down below their waists. One of them—a big, muscular type—had a biker's black scarf around his head, and the other three had hair hanging down to their shoulders. They called to her, making her heart pound, but she didn't respond. "This is all I need!" she thought. She put her left hand on her earphones, as if to tell them she hadn't heard, and carried on to the bottom of the stairs. She heard all four of them yelling and laughing behind her.

"Hey, baby, can't find your mommy?"

"C'mon. We'll give you a free ride."

"Yeah. Don't worry about Mr. Muscles here. He's a pussycat really."

She picked up her pace, and reached the ticket barrier. She was still unsure if it was the right one, but there were no signs and no one to ask. She put her ticket in the machine and walked through just as the four young men jumped over the neighboring barriers. She pretended not to notice them and headed for the platform, while the four of them danced around her, yelling and making gestures at her that she didn't understand. She turned around and saw two policemen behind the ticket barrier. She sighed with relief and rushed toward them, moving back through the exit barrier. None of the four followed.

"Excuse me!"

Neither of the cops, who were talking to one another, replied. She went up closer to them and said again, "Excuse me!"

They looked at her. She started to tell them that she was lost, wanted to go to Penn Station in New York, that she was Egyptian, that there were some young men frightening her, and that she didn't know where the last train went from. Her voice was strained and she sounded out of breath. One of the cops smiled at her and said in a slow, clear voice, "Young lady, why don't you take a minute to compose yourself and then tell us what you need?"

He carried on talking to his colleague. She looked over to the platform and saw the four young men looking at her and laughing. She thought for a minute, then took a deep breath. Her mother had once told her that keeping calm was the most important thing in such situations. She calmed herself as much as she could, and decided to focus on the most important thing. It was clear that the two cops would not get her home, so she had to find the train. Maybe she could get them to accompany her to the train.

"I'm lost. Looking for the train to Penn Station, New York. Can you help me?"

"Ah, now you're making sense. Yes, that's the platform you want: the one you just came out of. Hurry up, and remember the station is closed, and this is the last train in or out tonight."

"Can you come with me? I'm afraid of those four on the platform."

"Why? What did they do? Did any of them threaten you? Do you want to make a complaint?"

"No, I just want to get back to New York, but they're scaring me."

"You shouldn't be afraid if they haven't threatened you."

"But what they are doing and the gestures they've been making scared me."

"Miss, what do you suggest we do? Provide you with an escort home?"

She felt like she was choking again when she heard a commotion coming from the platform, turned around, and saw the front of the train come onto the platform. The two cops looked at her with a mixture of puzzlement and disdain. She looked over at the four young men waving to her to hurry up and catch the train. The train pulled in and the doors opened. She looked back and forth between the two cops walking away and the four guys, then ran to the train. The machine at the barrier wouldn't accept her ticket this time, so she jumped over without thinking, bags and all, and ran for the train, with the four young men still standing there, clapping their encouragement to her. She heard one of the cops yelling after her but she was already at the doors of the train so she got on, followed by the four young men. The doors closed and the train pulled away.

The train car was almost empty. She looked out of the corner of her eye and could only see three other passengers in the car. There was an older guy, who kept looking around the train car and who looked worn down by life somehow, and two men in ragged clothes sitting separately at the far end of the car. Every thirty seconds or so, one of them sipped from a bottle wrapped in a paper bag. A little flustered, she took her cell phone out to call her grandfather again. As it rang, she glanced at the four out of the corner of her eye, pretending to have it all together while internally she pleaded that her old grandpa would answer.

"Grandpa!"

"Hello, Salma."

"Look, I have had serious problems since I last spoke to you."

"Serious problems? Where are you?"

She quickly told him the whole story. He told her to calm down, saying it was easy to feel scared as a girl alone in a train station or among young men, but it was all in her head.

"Act naturally, and they'll act naturally with you."

"Naturally? No, you don't understand. These guys are really scary. I'm really frightened."

"Well don't be, my girl. Keep your head up. You'll be in Penn Station in five minutes. Then get a taxi and come straight over."

She called Aunt Amira. It rang once before she answered: "Yes, sweetie, where are you? I was worried about you. Haven't you gotten in yet?"

"I'm scared, Aunt Amira."

Amira tried to calm her down. After a little sobbing and crying, Salma pulled herself together. She explained what had happened, and immediately felt that her aunt understood her, unlike the two cops or even her grandfather. She just mentioned four big guys and Aunt Amira understood right away. She said that the station was dark and Amira knew exactly how she felt. Amira warned her to be really careful, because she didn't know what these men wanted with her.

"So what do I do?"

"Don't let any of them near you. If any of them touches you, hit back at him straightaway, OK? Hit him with anything you've got, and hit him in the place it'll hurt him most. Don't hesitate or be afraid. Hit him and scream 'Fire!' as loud as you can and pull the emergency brake. Do it all at the same time and don't be afraid. This will scare them and they'll run."

"OK. If any of them does anything, I'll do that."

"Don't wait until one does something. If any of them goes near you, you do it. If they sense you're weak they will have no mercy. Haven't you got pepper spray with you?"

"What is that?"

"My God, I don't know how your father and grandfather can let you travel around on your own like that."

Then the cell phone died on her.

The train car jerked around on its wheels, and the noise got louder when they went through tunnels, seeming suffocating to Salma.

The four men were talking to each other and to her, pointing and waving their arms around faster and faster. She turned her music up. She didn't hear everything they said, but worked out innuendos, along with the occasional obscene gesture. She'd seen this kind of thing in movies, usually just before the perpetrator attacked their victim. Wust El Balad ended, and the Black Eyed Peas came on next, reverberating through her ears. She was crying inside with terror, wondering what would happen next. Would they take her money, her camera, her whole bag? Or would they abduct and rape her, or kill her, or all of those things in that order? She had a lot of cash on her: about five hundred dollars. It was what remained from what her father had given her, and she had taken it with her from New York to Washington, but hadn't needed to spend it in the end. She wondered whether they would leave her alone if she gave them the money. But what if they thought she had more? She should give them her whole bag right off. But what about her camera, and all the pictures she'd taken on the trip? How could she go back to Egypt without a single picture? No one would believe her if she said they'd all been stolen.

Her thoughts were racing. "To hell with the pictures. To hell with this whole trip. Why did I come to America in the first place? Why didn't I spend the summer with Mom on the north coast?

"Mahmoud was right to be mad at me. He told me wanting to see the world, discover a new culture, see America on my own was a bad idea, and that I should wait until we could travel together. He had asked if Mom was for me traveling, or whether it had been Dad's idea. I hadn't replied. He'd said that if he'd been my father, he would never have let me travel alone.

"Maybe Dad did want to let me go, but it was me who really pushed for it when Grandpa mentioned it to Mom on the phone. I pestered them both until they agreed. What if these animals try to rape me now? None of the three in this train car is going to stop them; by the looks of them, they can barely look after themselves. Could I hold them off if they did attack me? Maybe if I do like Aunt Amira said and hit one of them where it really hurts, it might put the others off. Maybe they'll run off. What if they don't, though? Or what if they are just messing around and don't really mean to hurt me? Maybe they just want to scare me or make fun of me.

"Maybe I should give in. If they are going to rape me anyway, wouldn't it be better just to let them? Maybe they won't hurt me then. Maybe I can fool them into thinking I'm going along with it and buy myself some time to escape. But if I do that and can't escape in the end, what would this make me? Isn't it better to resist, or at least try to? How could I face my family and friends after that? How would Dad react? Maybe he'd console me and tell me it was a terrible experience, but something to learn from. What would Aunt Amira and her husband say when they found out? They had both been so against me going to Washington alone. Why didn't I listen to them?

"And Mahmoud: would he still want me after all this, or would he dump me? Even if he didn't leave me, could I stay with him, knowing what he'd be thinking? And my girlfriends at university: what would they say behind my back? No, I couldn't carry on living after something like that. Better to fight back, even if they kill me."

Salma's heart sank deeper with every passing second, and she sensed her own weakness more and more. She wanted to break down and cry and tell them to leave her alone, but she pretended to have it all together, and looked straight ahead of her as if they didn't exist. Her ignoring them made them even wilder and their fooling around turned into frustration, and then real anger. In her head, she prayed none of them would touch her. One of them put his hand on her bag, so she gave him a hard stare, and he pretended to be frightened of her. She prayed they wouldn't touch her and kept her hand in her coat pocket, clutching her pen like a knife.

She kept her hand in her pocket as the train pulled into a station, unsure if it was Penn, New York. She was looking out of the corner of her eye at the platform, when suddenly the muscular guy put his arm around her shoulder and whispered something in her ear she didn't hear. She tried to shrug him off, but he held on to her. There was no longer any room for doubt. She had to do something immediately. He brought his face close to hers, so she took her hand out of her pocket and with the full force of her anger and fear plunged the pen into his face. She didn't know where it lodged exactly. The train pulled into the station while the boy rolled around on the floor, screaming and holding his face. She could see blood flowing from him, while the other three, half shocked and half stupefied, stared at him. She ran out through the opening train car door and looked around for the name of the station as she ran along the platform. It wasn't Penn, New York. She heard them yelling and cursing at her. She heard the warning signal that the doors were closing, so she jumped into the next train car along. The doors closed before the boys could get in, leaving them hammering on the window and shouting threats at her. The wounded one had his hand to his eye and his face was covered in blood. She stared at them, tears streaming from her eyes. She wished she could have kicked them all to the floor. She gave them the finger, the one obscene gesture she knew, while she stood there separated from them by the glass window. She heard their threats and insults through the small, window that was open at the top. She stretched to try and close it, but felt cold metal against her skin. A blade glinted in the window's reflection. As the train pulled away, she saw one of them standing on the platform, a switchblade in his hand hanging by his side, while the other two dragged their wounded buddy along behind them: a scene she would never forget.

She hesitantly felt for the wound on her face, afraid to look at her reflection in the window. The train went through another dark tunnel. Blood covered her cheek and she felt it trickle down her face, sticky, warm, and thick. She wiped it off with her sleeve without thinking and tried to read the map pasted on the side of the train car. Penn Station was next. The train was completely empty apart from her. She curled up on a seat and stared at the tunnel walls through the window, then at the tracks, aimlessly, trying to ignore the blood rolling down her face. But it was getting worse. The train slowed as it entered the station, and a large sign loomed into view: "Penn Station." She got up quickly, making herself dizzy, and gripped the metal handles of the train-car door. She got straight out onto the platform when the train stopped, and ran toward the main concourse.

The train moved off and she was buffeted by the air, but all she felt was a mounting lightheadedness. It occurred to her that it must be almost midnight, and that she was about to turn twenty-one, the magical age she never believed she'd reach. Then again, maybe she'd been right; maybe she never would. Maybe she'd fall on the floor right then, dragged down by her faintness and the remorseless flow of blood. Her strength was rapidly dwindling. She didn't know what was going to happen to her. Maybe she should stop running, find a phone, and contact her grandfather or Aunt Amira. But they wouldn't get there in time. She was going to pass out soon; there was no doubt about it. Maybe she'd fall on the train tracks, or down the side of a train, or right there on the platform. Some criminal or other would slice her up and sell her body parts; maybe he'd rape her first.

"This is the end then," she said to herself. "You came all this way for it all to end here, a twenty-one-year-old corpse on a Penn Station platform."

She stopped running, or at least she thought she did. She tried to see where the exit was, but could only see floating forms and pulsing lights from different angles.

Seconds later, the world darkened in her eyes and she sank to the ground.

Author's Acknowledgments

I WOULD LIKE TO THANK Asmaa Abdallah, whose insightful reading and advice took this novel by the hand from its inception to its present form.